CLASSIC STORIES FROM
THE AGE OF DECADENCE

More short stories available
from Macmillan Collector's Library

Secrets in the Snow & Other Christmas Crime Stories
Classic Railway Stories
Classic Horror Stories
Classic Stories of the Sea
Classic Fantasy Stories
Classic Love Stories
Enchanted Tales
Classic Christmas Crime Stories
Women of the Harlem Renaissance: Poems & Stories
Classic Science Fiction Stories
Standing Her Ground: Classic Short Stories by Trailblazing Women
Classic Dog Stories
Classic Cat Stories

CLASSIC STORIES FROM THE AGE OF DECADENCE

Edited and introduced by
JANE DESMARAIS

MACMILLAN COLLECTOR'S LIBRARY

This collection first published 2025 by Macmillan Collector's Library
an imprint of Pan Macmillan
The Smithson, 6 Briset Street, London EC1M 5NR
EU representative: Macmillan Publishers Ireland Ltd,
1st Floor, The Liffey Trust Centre, 117–126 Sheriff Street Upper,
Dublin 1 D01 YC43
Associated companies throughout the world

ISBN 978-1-0350-5278-3

Selection copyright © Macmillan Publishers International Ltd. 2025
Introduction copyright © Jane Desmarais 2025

The permissions acknowledgements on p. 281 constitute an extension of this copyright page.

All rights reserved. No part of this publication may be reproduced, stored in a retrieval system, or transmitted, in any form, or by any means (including, without limitation, electronic, mechanical, photocopying, recording or otherwise) without the prior written permission of the publisher.

1 3 5 7 9 8 6 4 2

A CIP catalogue record for this book is available from the British Library.

Endpaper pattern by Andrew Davidson
Typeset in Plantin by Jouve (UK), Milton Keynes
Printed and bound in China by Imago

This book is sold subject to the condition that it shall not, by way of trade or otherwise, be lent, hired out, or otherwise circulated without the publisher's prior consent in any form of binding or cover other than that in which it is published and without a similar condition including this condition being imposed on the subsequent publisher. The publisher does not authorize the use or reproduction of any part of this book in any manner for the purpose of training artificial intelligence technologies or systems. The publisher expressly reserves this book from the Text and Data Mining exception in accordance with Article 4(3) of the European Union Digital Single Market Directive 2019/790.

The text of this book remains true to the original in every way and is reflective of the language and period in which it was originally written. Readers should be aware that there may be hurtful or indeed harmful phrases and terminology that were prevalent at the time these stories were written and in the context of the historical setting of these stories. Macmillan believes changing the text to reflect today's world would undermine the authenticity of the original, so has chosen to leave the text in its entirety. This does not, however, constitute an endorsement of the characterization, content or language used.

Visit **www.panmacmillan.com** to read more
about all our books and to buy them.

Contents

Introduction vii

ALGERNON CHARLES SWINBURNE 1
Dead Love

OSCAR WILDE 9
The Nightingale and the Rose

VERNON LEE 21
Dionea

JEAN LORRAIN 67
*Funeral Oration (*Oraison funèbre*)*

ERNEST DOWSON 77
A Case of Conscience

NETTA SYRETT 97
Thy Heart's Desire

LIONEL JOHNSON 135
Tobacco Clouds

ELLA D'ARCY 149
The Death Mask

GEORGE EGERTON 163
A Cross Line

KATE CHOPIN 195
An Egyptian Cigarette

MAX BEERBOHM 203
Enoch Soames
A Memory of the Eighteen-Nineties

RICHARD BRUCE NUGENT 253
Smoke, Lilies and Jade

Permissions Acknowledgements 281

Introduction

JANE DESMARAIS

'Draw the curtains, kindle a joss-stick in a dark corner,' John Betjeman enjoins us in his preface to *The 1890s: A Period Anthology in Prose and Verse* (1948), 'settle down on a sofa by the fire, light an Egyptian cigarette and sip a brandy and soda, as you think yourself back to the world which ended in prison and disgrace for Wilde, suicide for Crackanthorpe and John Davidson, premature death for Beardsley, Dowson, Lionel Johnson, religion for some, drink and drugs for others, temporary or permanent oblivion for many more'. As this post-war reverie suggests, the word 'decadence' has powerful associations with languid and unconventional refinement. It has enjoyed an intermittently strong currency for more than a hundred years, which continues still today. Decadence is associated with luxury, beauty, (dis)taste, but also degeneration, decay and disgust. On a broad level, it describes moral, political, cultural and historical decline, but from a more individual and personal perspective, it tends to be a clichéd term describing what is essentially luxurious self-indulgence. And so, we might talk about the decadence of eating a rich chocolate dessert ('chocolate decadence' as one restaurant menu has described it) or soaking in a hot bath decorated with rose petals.

In the ordinary sense, decadence is a common byword for 'naughty', but when we think of it in literary terms, it becomes much richer and more fascinating than the cliché might lead us to think. When 'decadence' is applied to literature and art, it can elude clear definition, because although it can refer to 'naughty' self-indulgent behaviour it also signals a contradictory array of ideas that have less to do with lazy excess than with notions of transgression, corruption, exoticism and perversion. All of these are key characteristics of civilizations in decline. To refer to something as decadent is to reach back to the classical past and the idea of 'The Decadence', a period of alleged literary and linguistic decline associated with the fall of the Roman empire (AD 476) and a gallery of repugnant emperors, and forwards to our own times of political corruption, social degeneracy and personal excess.

Often emerging as a mood (perfectly evoked by Oscar Wilde's 'The Nightingale and the Rose' (1888)) – discontinuous but recurrent, and powerful while its presence lasts – decadence is an expansive tradition in literature. There is no single defining trajectory of ideas; instead, we find decadent moments as well as 'movements', decadent trails that lead nowhere in particular, and decadent residues in other more well-defined areas such as late Romanticism, Naturalism, Symbolism and Modernism. Strange to think that at the end of the nineteenth century decadent preoccupations were the focus of what Holbrook Jackson described in *The Eighteen Nineties* (1913) as 'a movement of elderly youths who wrote themselves out in a slender volume or so of hot verse or ornate prose, and slipped away to die in taverns and gutters', but although these writers were relatively few in number and mostly male, their work went against the grain, challenging expectations about 'good' art, paving the way for literary modernism.

At a time when political, cultural and scientific revolutions had swept across Europe, when social change seemed to be accelerating towards a state of affairs of which no one could be fully certain, late nineteenth-century decadent writers – much like their Roman forebears – envisaged history in biological terms, as a series of life cycles, where youth and maturity ultimately fade and decline. In their work we repeatedly encounter highly sensual images of beauty and rot, decrepitude and disease, cruelty and sterility. Disgusted by metropolitan landscapes of overcrowding and poverty, and revolted by the impact of industrialization and the new commercial culture, aesthetes and decadents found in sensory and often sexual experience an escape from the evil of banality, and in acts of private sensual indulgence they identified a way of shocking the complacent and culturally deodorized middle classes. They were connoisseurs of the opium pipe and passing cloud. Flux, filth and all manner of sensual excitements were their obsessions. In their writings, Nature is represented as a figure of treacherous transience. Ripening and rotting, individuals must prepare themselves for a life, 'burn[ing] always with a hard, gemlike flame' (to borrow Walter Pater's phrase), which then flickers and disappears.

In France, where the decadent tradition reached a peak in the 1880s, there were two associated concepts: *décadence* and *décadentisme*. The first is a historical and material signifier, and refers to the process of decay, or falling away and decline, as we might find in civilizations or buildings (deriving from the Latin term *de* + *cadere*, to fall away from). The second, rarer usage, *décadentisme*, refers to a style or an aesthetic, and is a correlate of terms like Symbolism or Parnassianism, which refer to a particular movement or school of writers. *Décadisme* is another, but rarely used, variant coined by Anatole

Introduction

Baju in the late 1880s and famously cited by Paul Verlaine in *Le Figaro* of 4 April 1891 as an alternative to the term 'symbolism'. In the nineteenth century the French term *décadence* was used by various European writers, artists, philosophers and critics as a way of pinning the term to its French cultural roots. It was used to suggest sophistication. Friedrich Nietzsche used it in this way (usually in a pejorative sense that he applied to Christianity), and so did the artist Aubrey Beardsley, though his positive embrace of French sophistication was also intended as a provocation to the English Old Guard who disliked his work. While 'Frenchness' in the late nineteenth century was for many English critics synonymous with lax morals and social and sexual deviance, for a few its use connoted a modern outlook and was a sign to others that cross-cultural influences were to be welcomed.

At the fin de siècle, London had superseded Paris as the cosmopolitan centre of decadence, where a small number of writers, artists and publishers frequented fashionable cafes, like St James's (known as 'Jimmy's') in Piccadilly, London, to dress up, drink cocktails and discuss the new literature. The decadent publishing scene was dominated by two publishing houses, The Bodley Head run by John Lane and a seedier outfit a few streets away run by the pornographic bookseller Leonard Smithers, and their two rather short-lived journals, *The Yellow Book* (1894–7) and *The Savoy* (1896). Three of the stories in this selection were published in Lane's *The Yellow Book*. Netta Syrett's 'Thy Heart's Desire' (1894) highlights the role of women at the fin de siècle; Lionel Johnson's 'Tobacco Clouds' (1894), together with Kate Chopin's 'An Egyptian Cigarette' (1900), are fusions of story, meditation and reverie; and Ella D'Arcy's 'The Death Mask' (1896) is a homage to Wilde's *The Picture of Dorian Gray* (1890). Syrett and D'Arcy were among a number of New Women writers who advanced their careers by publishing in *The Yellow Book*, which as Talia Schaffer notes in her book *The Forgotten Female Aesthetes: Literary Culture in Late-Victorian England* (2000) 'positioned women's writing as an integral part of aestheticism'.

At the end of the nineteenth century, the term 'decadence' was a fashionable epithet in London literary circles and connoted 'Frenchness' and moral laxity. Its two living symbols, Wilde and Beardsley, consciously cultivated a continental and decadent persona, with the intention of clashing with the prevailing nationalistic ideal in British culture. 'Beardsley is a Decadent, and must do as the Decadents do', sighed *The Magazine of Art* in 1897, 'nations ripe and ripe, and when they rot and rot,

Introduction

decadence is the tale that hangs thereby'. In France at the fin de siècle, the term lost some of its original protesting resonance and became subsumed under the notional auspices of Symbolism, but in England, it was used as a convenient critical tool with which to effect moral rather than literary or artistic censure. In Germany, by contrast, the term 'decadence' acquired a different set of connotations. It was mobilized most significantly by Max Nordau in his major study *Entartung* (1892) to pathologize the art of the avant-garde. By the time the English translation, *Degeneration*, appeared in 1895, decadence was synonymous with the idea of entropic decline, and decay became the prevailing flavour of the 1890s.

The fin de siècle was shaped by critics into a period piece as the 'decadent', the 'naughty', 'yellow' nineties ('mauve' in the United States), beautifully captured in Max Beerbohm's comic tragedy about an aspiring poet Enoch Soames, titled 'Enoch Soames: A Memory of the Eighteen-Nineties' (1916). Beerbohm's story is set in the mid 1890s, the heyday of the 'Beardsley Period' as he called it, but by 1897 the decade was losing some of its decadent resonance. Fin-de-siècle decadence was as insubstantial as cigarette smoke, but a faint aroma lingered on into the early twentieth century. Orlo

Williams, writing in *The London Mercury* in 1920, referred to the 'ripe, romantic flavour' of the decade as:

> like that of some departed and not too outrageously Bohemian relative referred to by elders with an indulgent smile and shake of the head as 'your poor uncle Roger', the exact nature of whose extravagances is wrapped in a golden haze, and over whose faded photograph in the family album a glamour is cast – more glamour, perhaps, than his mortal presence ever gave out in its heyday.

Decadent fiction properly emerged in France with *Contes Cruels* (1883) by Auguste Villiers de l'Isle-Adam (1838–89), and it is clearly a product of Edgar Allan Poe's macabre sensationalism in the short story form, although adapted to a more sophisticated readership. In Villiers's story 'The Eleventh-Hour Guest' (not included in this selection), Poe's morbid obsessions are woven into a fictional world of languid Parisian elegance, of idle debauchees supping flirtatiously with courtesans, that chimes with the new decadent sensibility. The indebtedness of decadent fiction to Poe's Gothic formula appears frequently in the form of such motifs as deadly curses and contagions, which echo

Introduction

Poe's own 'The Mask of the Red Death' through to Rachilde's 'The Grape-Harvest of Sodom' (also not included in this selection but available in translation). A similar curse-like motif recurs as the secret vice, which is narcotic in Jean Lorrain's 'Funeral Oration' ('*Oraison funèbre*', 1891). Decadent stories are often disturbing and unsettling, a quality they share with horror fiction, ghost stories and fantasy, as well as Gothic literature. Vernon Lee's 'Dionea' (1890), which brings Pygmalionism into weird play with *femme fatale* tropes, produces shivers while Ernest Dowson's 'A Case of Conscience' (1891), a narrative about a young girl's internal conflict between love and moral duty, is unsettling in a different way.

In general, the newly distinctive element that decadent writers brought to prose fiction was their emphasis on sexuality and sexual perversity. Whereas in the detective and Gothic traditions deriving from Poe, the dark secret of the narrative tended to be murder or insanity, in decadent fiction it was more often revealed to be an 'abnormality' of the erotic life: necrophilia in Algernon Charles Swinburne's deliciously morbid and perverse tale 'Dead Love' (1864) and bi-sexuality, which was widely seen as an abnormality at the time, in Richard Bruce Nugent's tale 'Smoke, Lilies, and Jade' (1926) set in

Harlem, New York City. The figure of the *femme fatale* and the modern woman are recurring preoccupations, the latter especially in the work of women writers such as George Egerton, whose 'A Cross Line' from the collection *Keynotes* (1898) explores desire and sex outside marriage.

As this selection shows, decadent fiction as a genre, both in its long and short forms, is pleasurably elusive. It may be understood in general terms as an unstable compound of Gothic or horror-story ingredients with elements of lurid eroticism and of glamorous 'high-society' setting and characterization. However, as we discover, in any individual work the balance of these elements varies, and the prime example of this is, of course, the macabre melodramatic plot of Wilde's prose romance *The Picture of Dorian Gray*, which sits uneasily both with its attempts to announce a new 'way of life' in the aphorisms and aesthetic doctrines of Lord Henry Wotton, and with its coded homoerotic implications.

In many senses, Jackson was right. Decadence was a 'movement of elderly youths', who in the 1880s and 1890s mounted an ultimately flaccid resistance against authority and orthodoxy. Many, if not most, were bourgeois, and some even had pretensions towards the aristocracy; yet despite this,

Introduction

they remained vigorously opposed to the establishment and to the complacency and conservatism of bourgeois taste, while at the same time representing exactly that – middle-class taste. In treating subjects that were taboo and adopting a decadent style of writing that was ornate and sensual, these writers both honoured and deconstructed contemporary cultural idealism of the past and drew repeatedly upon ancient myths and archaic structures to express perverse aspects of modernity. In their generically hybrid short fiction, they work a passage between unsettling, spine-tingling Gothic horror and fairy-tale fantasy and aesthetic prose, they use the form provocatively to question conventional boundaries of gender and sexuality, and create sensualized fiction that imitates the act of meditation or state of transcendence through intoxication.

The wisps of smoke that curl and filter through the stories in this collection are an invitation to lie back and release the soul and imagination. Just like the blue smoke wafting from the 'ivory holder inlaid with red jade and green' in Nugent's stream-of-consciousness narrative, we should open our minds to experience new realms of fantasy and desire. And so, let's draw those curtains and follow Betjeman's bidding . . . 'Another sip of brandy and another

Egyptian cigarette; a whiff of opium perhaps and we can see the mood of the time. Carriages from Mayfair to Belgravia, sun-blinds on verandahs in Park Lane, stable-smells in the mews behind, and stretching in front of us the plane-trees, the grass, the pedestrians and the riders in the Park . . .'

CLASSIC STORIES FROM THE
AGE OF DECADENCE

ALGERNON CHARLES SWINBURNE

Dead Love

About the time of the great troubles in France, that fell out between the parties of Armagnac and of Burgundy, there was slain in a fight in Paris a follower of the Duke John, who was a good knight called Messire Jacques d'Aspremont. This Jacques was a very fair and strong man, hardy of his hands, and before he was slain he did many things wonderful and of great courage, and forty of the folk of the other party he slew, and many of these were great captains, of whom the chief and the worthiest was Messire Olivier de Bois-Percé; but at last he was shot in the neck with an arrow, so that between the nape and the apple the flesh was cleanly cloven in twain. And when he was dead his men drew forth his body of the fierce battle, and covered it with a fair woven cloak. Then the people of Armagnac, taking good heart because of his death, fell the more heavily upon his followers, and slew very many of them. And a certain soldier, named Amaury de Jacqueville, whom they called Courtebarbe, did best of all that party; for, crying out with a great noise, "Sus, sus!" he brought up the men after him, and threw them forward into the hot part of the fighting, where there was a sharp clamour; and this Amaury, laughing and crying out as a man that took a great delight in such matters of war, made of himself more noise with smiting and with shouting than any ten, and they of Burgundy were astonished and beaten down. And when he was weary, and his men had got the upper hand of those of Burgundy, he left off slaying, and beheld where Messire d'Aspremont was covered up with his cloak; and he lay just across the door of Messire Olivier, whom the said Jacques had slain, who was also a cousin of Amaury's. Then said Amaury:

"Take up now the body of this dead fellow, and carry it into the house; for my cousin Madame Yolande shall have great delight to behold the face of the fellow dead by whom her husband has got his end, and it shall make the tiding sweeter to her."

So they took up this dead knight Messire Jacques, and carried him into a fair chamber lighted with broad windows, and herein sat the wife of Olivier, who was called Yolande de Craon, and she was akin far off to Pierre de Craon, who would have slain the Constable. And Amaury said to her:

"Fair and dear cousin, and my good lady, we give

you for your husband slain the body of him that slew my cousin; make the best cheer that you may, and comfort yourself that he has found a good death and a good friend to do justice on his slayer; for this man was a good knight, and I that have revenged him account myself none of the worst."

And with this Amaury and his people took leave of her. Then Yolande, being left alone, began at first to weep grievously, and so much that she was heavy and weary; and afterward she looked upon the face of Jacques d'Aspremont, and held one of his hands with hers, and said:

"Ah, false thief and coward! it is great pity thou wert not hung on a gallows, who hast slain by treachery the most noble knight of the world, and to me the most loving and the faithfulest man alive, and that never did any discourtesy to any man, and was the most single and pure lover that ever a married lady had to be her knight; and never said any word to me but sweet words. Ah, false coward! there was never such a knight of thy kin."

Then, considering his face earnestly, she saw that it was a fair face enough, and by seeming the face of a good knight; and she repented of her bitter words, saying with herself:

"Certainly this one, too, was a good man and valiant," and was sorry for his death.

And she pulled out the arrow-head that was broken, and closed up the wound of his neck with ointments. And then beholding his dead open eyes, she fell into a great torrent of weeping, so that her tears fell all over his face and throat. And all the time of this bitter sorrow she thought how goodly a man this Jacques must have been in his life, who being dead had such power upon her pity. And for compassion of his great beauty she wept so exceedingly and long that she fell down upon his body in a swoon, embracing him, and so lay the space of two hours with her face against his; and being awaked she had no other desire but only to behold him again, and so all that day neither ate nor slept at all, but for the most part lay and wept. And afterward, out of her love, she caused the body of this knight to be preserved with spice, and made him a golden coffin open at the top, and clothed him with the fairest clothes she could get, and had this coffin always by her bed in her chamber. And when this was done she sat down over against him and held his arms about her neck, weeping, and she said:

"Ah, Jacques! although alive I was not worthy, so that I never saw the beauty and goodness of your living body with my sorrowful eyes, yet now being dead, I thank God that I have this grace to behold you. Alas, Jacques! you have no sight now to discern what things are beautiful, therefore you may now love me as well as another, for with dead men there is no difference of women. But, truly, although I were the fairest of all Christian women that now is, I were in nowise worthy to love you; nevertheless, have compassion upon me that for your sake have forgotten the most noble husband of the world."

And this Yolande, that made such complaining of love to a dead man, was one of the fairest ladies of all that time, and of great reputation; and there were many good men that loved her greatly, and would fain have had some favour at her hands; of whom she made no account, saying always, that her dead lover was better than many lovers living. Then certain people said that she was bewitched; and one of these was Amaury. And they would have taken the body to burn it, that the charm might be brought to an end; for they said that a demon had entered in and taken it in possession; which she hearing fell into extreme rage, and said that if her lover were alive, there was not so good a knight among them, that he should undertake the charge of that saying; at which speech of hers there was great laughter.

And upon a night there came into her house Amaury and certain others, that were minded to see this matter for themselves. And no man kept the doors; for all her people had gone away, saving only a damsel that remained with her; and the doors stood open, as in a house where there is no man. And they stood in the doorway of her chamber, and heard her say this that ensues:—

"O most fair and perfect knight, the best that ever was in any time of battle, or in any company of ladies, and the most courteous man, have pity upon me, most sorrowful woman and handmaid. For in your life you had some other lady to love you, and were to her a most true and good lover; but now you have none other but me only, and I am not worthy that you should so much as kiss me on my sad lips, wherein is all this lamentation. And though your own lady were the fairer and the more worthy, yet consider, for God's pity and mine, how she has forgotten the love of your body and the kindness of your espousals, and lives easily with some other man, and is wedded to him with all honour; but I have neither ease nor honour, and yet I am your true maiden and servant."

And then she embraced and kissed him many times. And Amaury was very wroth, but he refrained himself: and his friends were troubled and full of wonder. Then they beheld how she held his body between her arms, and kissed him in the neck with all her strength; and after a certain time it seemed to them that the body of Jacques moved and sat up;

and she was no whit amazed, but rose up with him, embracing him. And Jacques said to her:

"I beseech you, now that you would make a covenant with me, to love me always."

And she bowed her head suddenly, and said nothing.

Then said Jacques:

"Seeing you have done so much for love of me, we twain shall never go in sunder: and for this reason has God given back to me the life of my mortal body."

And after this they had the greatest joy together, and the most perfect solace that may be imagined: and she sat and beheld him, and many times fell into a little quick laughter for her great pleasure and delight.

Then came Amaury suddenly into the chamber, and caught his sword into his hand, and said to her:

"Ah, wicked leman, now at length is come the end of thy horrible love and of thy life at once;" and smote her through the two sides with his sword, so that she fell down, and with a great sigh full unwillingly delivered up her spirit, which was no sooner fled out of her perishing body, but immediately the soul departed also out of the body of her lover, and he became as one that had been all those days dead.

And the next day the people caused their two

bodies to be burned openly in the place where witches were used to be burned: and it is reported by some that an evil spirit was seen to come out of the mouth of Jacques d'Aspremont, with a most pitiful cry, like the cry of a hurt beast. By which thing all men knew that the soul of this woman, for the folly of her sinful and most strange affection, was thus evidently given over to the delusion of the evil one and the pains of condemnation.

Oscar Wilde

The Nightingale and the Rose

'She said that she would dance with me if I brought her red roses,' cried the young student, 'but in all my garden there is no red rose.'

From her nest in the holm-oak tree the nightingale heard him, and she looked out through the leaves and wondered.

'No red rose in all my garden!' he cried, and his beautiful eyes filled with tears. 'Ah, on what little things does happiness depend! I have read all that the wise men have written, and all the secrets of philosophy are mine, yet for want of a red rose is my life made wretched.'

'Here at last is a true lover,' said the nightingale. 'Night after night have I sung of him, though I knew him not; night after night have I told his story to the stars and now I see him. His hair is dark as the hyacinth-blossom, and his lips are red as the rose of his desire; but passion has made his face like pale ivory, and sorrow has set her seal upon his brow.'

'The prince gives a ball tomorrow night,' murmured the young student, 'and my love will be of the company. If I bring her a red rose she will dance with me till dawn. If I bring her a red rose, I shall hold her in my arms, and she will lean her head upon my shoulder, and her hand will be clasped in mine. But there is no red rose in my garden, so I shall sit lonely, and she will pass me by. She will have no heed of me, and my heart will break.'

'Here, indeed, is the true lover,' said the nightingale. 'What I sing of, he suffers; what is joy to me, to him is pain. Surely love is a wonderful thing. It is more precious than emeralds, and dearer than fine opals. Pearls and pomegranates cannot buy it, nor is it set forth in the market-place. It may not be purchased of the merchants, nor can it be weighed out in the balance for gold.'

'The musicians will sit in their gallery,' said the young student, 'and play upon their stringed instruments, and my love will dance to the sound of the harp and the violin. She will dance so lightly that her feet will not touch the floor, and the courtiers in their gay dresses will throng round her. But with me she will not dance, for I have no red rose to give her;' and he flung himself down on the grass, and buried his face in his hands, and wept.

The Nightingale and the Rose

'Why is he weeping?' asked a little green lizard as he ran past him with his tail in the air.

'Why, indeed!' said a butterfly, who was fluttering about after a sunbeam.

'Why, indeed?' whispered a daisy to his neighbour, in a soft, low voice.

'He is weeping for a red rose,' said the nightingale.

'For a red rose?' they cried; 'how very ridiculous!' and the little lizard, who was something of a cynic, laughed outright.

But the nightingale understood the secret of the student's sorrow, and she sat silent in the oak tree, and thought about the mystery of love.

Suddenly she spread her brown wings for flight, and soared into the air. She passed through the grove like a shadow and like a shadow she sailed across the garden.

In the centre of the grass-plot was standing a beautiful rose tree, and when she saw it she flew over to it, and lit upon a spray.

'Give me a red rose,' she cried, 'and I will sing you my sweetest song.'

But the tree shook its head. 'My roses are white,' it answered; 'as white as the foam of the sea, and whiter than the snow upon the mountain. But go to my brother who grows round the old sundial, and perhaps he will give you what you want.'

So the nightingale flew over to the rose tree that was growing round the old sundial.

'Give me a red rose,' she cried, 'and I will sing you my sweetest song.'

But the tree shook its head. 'My roses are yellow,' it answered; 'as yellow as the hair of the mermaiden who sits upon an amber throne, and yellower than the daffodil that blooms in the meadow before the mower comes with his scythe. But go to my brother who grows beneath the student's window, and perhaps he will give you what you want."

So the nightingale flew over to the rose tree that was growing beneath the student's window.

'Give me a red rose,' she cried, 'and I will sing you my sweetest song.'

But the tree shook its head.

'My roses are red,' it answered; 'as red as the feet of the dove, and redder than the great fans of coral that wave and wave in the ocean-cavern. But the winter has chilled my veins, and the frost has nipped my buds, and the storm has broken my branches, and I shall have no roses at all this year.'

'One red rose is all I want,' cried the nightingale, 'only one red rose! Is there no way by which I can get it?'

The Nightingale and the Rose

'There is a way,' answered the tree; 'but it is so terrible that I dare not tell it to you.'

'Tell it to me,' said the nightingale, 'I am not afraid.'

'If you want a red rose,' said the tree, 'you must build it out of music by moonlight, and stain it with your own heart's-blood. You must sing to me with your breast against a thorn. All night long you must sing to me, and the thorn must pierce your heart, and your life-blood must flow into my veins and become mine.'

'Death is a great price to pay for a red rose,' cried the nightingale, 'and life is very dear to all. It is pleasant to sit in the green wood, and to watch the sun in his chariot of gold, and the moon in her chariot of pearl. Sweet is the scent of the hawthorn, and sweet are the bluebells that hide in the valley, and the heather that blows on the hill. Yet love is better than life and what is the heart of a bird compared to the heart of a man?'

So she spread her brown wings for flight, and soared into the air. She swept over the garden like a shadow, and like a shadow she sailed through the grove.

The young student was still lying on the grass, where she had left him, and the tears were not yet dry in his beautiful eyes.

'Be happy,' cried the nightingale, 'be happy; you shall have your red rose. I will build it out of music by moonlight, and stain it with my own heart's-blood. All that I ask of you in return is that you will be a true lover, for Love is wiser than Philosophy, though he is wise, and mightier than Power, though he is mighty. Flame-coloured are his wings, and coloured like flame is his body. His lips are sweet as honey, and his breath is like frankincense.'

The student looked up from the grass, and listened, but he could not understand what the nightingale was saying to him, for he only knew the things that are written down in books.

But the oak tree understood, and felt sad for he was very fond of the little nightingale who had built her nest in his branches.

'Sing me one last song,' he whispered. 'I shall feel lonely when you are gone.'

So the nightingale sang to the oak tree, and her voice was like water bubbling from a silver jar.

When she had finished her song, the student got up, and pulled a notebook and a lead-pencil out of his pocket.

'She has form,' he said to himself, as he walked away through the grove – 'that cannot be denied to her; but has she got feeling? I am afraid not. In fact, she is like most artists; she is all style without any

The Nightingale and the Rose

sincerity. She would not sacrifice herself for others. She thinks merely of music, and everybody knows that the arts are selfish. Still, it must be admitted that she has some beautiful notes in her voice. What a pity it is that they do not mean anything, or do any practical good!' And he went into his room, and lay down on his little pallet-bed, and began to think of his love; and, after a time, he fell asleep.

And when the moon shone in the heavens the nightingale flew to the rose tree, and set her breast against the thorn. All night long she sang, with her breast against the thorn, and the cold crystal moon leaned down and listened. All night long she sang, and the thorn went deeper and deeper into her breast, and her lifeblood ebbed away from her.

She sang first of the birth of love in the heart of a boy and a girl. And on the topmost spray of the rose tree there blossomed a marvellous rose, petal following petal, as song followed song. Pale was it, at first, as the mist that hangs over the river – pale as the feet of the morning, and silver as the wings of the dawn. As the shadow of a rose in a mirror of silver, as the shadow of a rose in a water-pool, so was the rose that blossomed on the topmost spray of the tree.

But the tree cried to the nightingale to press

closer against the thorn. 'Press closer, little nightingale,' cried the tree, 'or the day will come before the rose is finished.'

So the nightingale pressed closer against the thorn and louder and louder grew her song, for she sang of the birth of passion in the soul of a man and a maid.

And a delicate flush of pink came into the leaves of the rose, like the flush in the face of the bridegroom when he kisses the lips of the bride. But the thorn had not yet reached her heart, so the rose's heart remained white, for only a nightingale's heart's-blood can crimson the heart of a rose.

And the tree cried to the nightingale to press closer against the thorn. 'Press closer, little nightingale,' cried the tree, 'or the day will come before the rose is finished.'

So the nightingale pressed closer against the thorn, and the thorn touched her heart, and a fierce pang of pain shot through her. Bitter, bitter was the pain, and wilder and wilder grew her song, for she sang of the love that is perfected by death, of the love that dies not in the tomb.

And the marvellous rose became crimson, like the rose of the eastern sky. Crimson was the girdle of petals, and crimson as a ruby was the heart.

But the nightingale's voice grew fainter, and her

The Nightingale and the Rose

little wings began to beat, and a film came over her eyes. Fainter and fainter grew her song, and she felt something choking her in her throat.

Then she gave one last burst of music. The white moon heard it, and she forgot the dawn, and lingered on in the sky. The red rose heard it, and it trembled all over with ecstasy, and opened its petals to the cold morning air. Echo bore it to her purple cavern in the hills, and woke the sleeping shepherds from their dreams. It floated through the reeds of the river, and they carried its message to the sea.

'Look, look!' cried the tree, 'the rose is finished now;' but the nightingale made no answer, for she was lying dead in the long grass, with the thorn in her heart.

And at noon the student opened his window and looked out.

'Why what a wonderful piece of luck,' he cried; 'here is a red rose! I have never seen any rose like it in all my life. It is so beautiful that I am sure it has a long Latin name;' and he leaned down and plucked it.

Then he put on his hat, and ran up to the professor's house with the rose in his hand.

The daughter of the professor was sitting in the

doorway winding blue silk on a reel, and her little dog was lying at her feet.

'You said that you would dance with me if I brought you a red rose,' cried the student. 'Here is the reddest rose in all the world. You will wear it tonight next your heart, and as we dance together it will tell you how I love you.'

But the girl frowned.

'I am afraid it will not go with my dress,' she answered; 'and, besides, the chamberlain's nephew has sent me some real jewels, and everybody knows that jewels cost far more than flowers.'

'Well, upon my word, you are very ungrateful,' said the student angrily; and he threw the rose into the street, where it fell into the gutter, and a cart-wheel went over it.

'Ungrateful!' said the girl. 'I tell you what, you are very rude; and, after all, who are you? Only a student. Why, I don't believe you have even got silver buckles to your shoes as the chamberlain's nephew has;' and she got up from her chair and went into the house.

'What a silly thing love is!' said the student as he walked away. 'It is not half as useful as logic, for it does not prove anything, and it is always telling one of things that are not going to happen, and making one believe things that are not true. In fact, it is quite unpractical, and, as in this age to be practical is everything, I shall go back to philosophy and study metaphysics.'

So he returned to his room and pulled out a great dusty book, and began to read.

VERNON LEE

Dionea

*From the Letters of Doctor Alessandro De Rosis
to the Lady Evelyn Savelli, Princess of Sabina.*

MONTEMIRTO LIGURE, *June* 29, 1873.
I take immediate advantage of the generous offer of your Excellency (allow an old Republican who has held you on his knees to address you by that title sometimes, 'tis so appropriate) to help our poor people. I never expected to come a-begging so soon. For the olive crop has been unusually plenteous. We semi-Genoese don't pick the olives unripe, like our Tuscan neighbours, but let them grow big and black, when the young fellows go into the trees with long reeds and shake them down on the grass for the women to collect—a pretty sight which your Excellency must see some day: the grey trees with the brown, barefoot lads craning, balanced in the branches, and the turquoise sea as background just beneath. . . . That sea of ours—it is all along of it that I wish to ask for money.

Looking up from my desk, I see the sea through the window, deep below and beyond the olive woods, bluish-green in the sunshine and veined with violet under the cloud-bars, like one of your Ravenna mosaics spread out as pavement for the world: a wicked sea, wicked in its loveliness, wickeder than your grey northern ones, and from which must have arisen in times gone by (when Phoenicians or Greeks built the temples at Lerici and Porto Venere) a baleful goddess of beauty, a Venus Verticordia, but in the bad sense of the word, overwhelming men's lives in sudden darkness like that squall of last week.

To come to the point. I want you, dear Lady Evelyn, to promise me some money, a great deal of money, as much as would buy you a little mannish cloth frock—for the complete bringing-up, until years of discretion, of a young stranger whom the sea has laid upon our shore. Our people, kind as they are, are very poor, and overburdened with children; besides, they have got a certain repugnance for this poor little waif, cast up by that dreadful storm, and who is doubtless a heathen, for she had no little crosses or scapulars on, like proper Christian children. So, being unable to get any of our women to adopt the child, and having an old bachelor's terror of my housekeeper, I have bethought me of certain nuns, holy women, who teach little girls to say their prayers and make lace close by here; and of your dear Excellency to pay for the whole business.

Poor little brown mite! She was picked up after the storm (such a set-out of ship-models and votive candles as that storm must have brought the Madonna at Porto Venere!) on a strip of sand between the rocks of our castle: the thing was really miraculous, for this coast is like a shark's jaw, and the bits of sand are tiny and far between. She was lashed to a plank, swaddled up close in outlandish garments; and when they brought her to me they thought she must certainly be dead: a little girl of four or five, decidedly pretty, and as brown as a berry, who, when she came to, shook her head to show she understood no kind of Italian, and jabbered some half-intelligible Eastern jabber, a few Greek words embedded in I know not what; the Superior of the College De Propagandâ Fidē would be puzzled to know. The child appears to be the only survivor from a ship which must have gone down in the great squall, and whose timbers have been strewing the bay for some days past; no one at Spezia or in any of our ports knows anything about her, but she was seen, apparently making for Porto Venere, by some of our sardine-fishers: a big, lumbering craft, with eyes painted on each side of the prow, which, as you know, is a peculiarity of Greek boats. She was sighted for the last time off the island of Palmaria, entering, with all sails spread, right into the thick of the storm-darkness. No bodies, strangely enough, have been washed ashore.

July 10.

I have received the money, dear Donna Evelina. There was tremendous excitement down at San Massimo when the carrier came in with a registered letter, and I was sent for, in presence of all the village authorities, to sign my name on the postal register.

The child has already been settled some days with the nuns; such dear little nuns (nuns always go straight to the heart of an old priest-hater and conspirator against the Pope, you know), dressed in brown robes and close, white caps, with an immense round straw-hat flapping behind their heads like a nimbus: they are called Sisters of the Stigmata, and have a convent and school at San Massimo, a little way inland, with an untidy garden full of lavender and cherry-trees. Your *protégée* has already half set the convent, the village, the Episcopal See, the Order of St. Francis, by the ears.

First, because nobody could make out whether or not she had been christened. The question was a grave one, for it appears (as your uncle-in-law, the Cardinal, will tell you) that it is almost equally undesirable to be christened twice over as not to be christened at all. The first danger was finally decided upon as the less terrible; but the child, they say, had evidently been baptized before, and knew that the operation ought not to be repeated, for she kicked and plunged and yelled like twenty little devils, and positively would not let the holy water touch her. The Mother Superior, who always took for granted that the baptism had taken place before, says that the child was quite right, and that Heaven was trying to prevent a sacrilege; but the priest and the barber's wife, who had to hold her, think the occurrence fearful, and suspect the little girl of being a Protestant. Then the question of the name. Pinned to her clothes—striped Eastern things, and that kind of crinkled silk stuff they weave in Crete and Cyprus—was a piece of parchment, a scapular we thought at first, but which was found to contain only the name Διονεα—Dionea, as they pronounce it here. The question was, Could such a name be fitly borne by a young lady at the Convent of the Stigmata? Half the population here have names as unchristian quite—Norma, Odoacer, Archimedes—my housemaid is called Themis—but Dionea seemed to scandalise every one, perhaps because these good folk had a mysterious instinct that the name is derived from Dione, one of the loves of Father Zeus, and mother of no less a lady than the goddess Venus. The child was very near being called Maria, although there are already twenty-three other Marias, Mariettas, Mariuccias, and so forth at the convent. But the sister-bookkeeper, who apparently detests monotony, bethought her to look out Dionea first in the Calendar, which proved useless; and then in a big vellum-bound book, printed at Venice in 1625, called "Flos Sanctorum, or Lives of the Saints, by Father Ribadeneira, S.J., with the addition of such Saints as have no assigned place in the Almanack, otherwise called the Movable or Extravagant Saints." The zeal of Sister Anna Maddalena has been rewarded, for there, among the Extravagant Saints, sure enough, with a border of palm-branches and hour-glasses, stands the name of Saint Dionea, Virgin and Martyr, a lady of Antioch, put to death by the Emperor Decius. I know your Excellency's taste for historical information, so I forward this item. But I fear, dear Lady Evelyn, I fear that the heavenly patroness of your little sea-waif was a much more extravagant saint than that.

Dionea

December 21, 1879.

Many thanks, dear Donna Evelina, for the money for Dionea's schooling. Indeed, it was not wanted yet: the accomplishments of young ladies are taught at a very moderate rate at Montemirto: and as to clothes, which you mention, a pair of wooden clogs, with pretty red tips, costs sixty-five centimes, and ought to last three years, if the owner is careful to carry them on her head in a neat parcel when out walking, and to put them on again only on entering the village. The Mother Superior is greatly overcome by your Excellency's munificence towards the convent, and much perturbed at being unable to send you a specimen of your *protégée*'s skill, exemplified in an embroidered pocket-handkerchief or a pair of mittens; but the fact is that poor Dionea *has* no skill. "We will pray to the Madonna and St. Francis to make her more worthy," remarked the Superior. Perhaps, however, your Excellency, who is, I fear but a Pagan woman (for all the Savelli Popes and St. Andrew Savelli's miracles), and insufficiently appreciative of embroidered pocket-handkerchiefs, will be quite as satisfied to hear that Dionea, instead of skill, has got the prettiest face of any little girl in Montemirto. She is tall, for her age (she is eleven) quite wonderfully well proportioned and extremely strong: of all the convent-full, she is the only one for whom I have never been called in. The features are very regular, the hair black, and despite all the good Sisters' efforts to keep it smooth like a Chinaman's, beautifully curly. I am glad she should be pretty, for she will more easily find a husband; and also because it seems fitting that your *protégée* should be beautiful. Unfortunately her character is not so satisfactory: she hates learning, sewing, washing up the dishes, all equally. I am sorry to say she shows no natural piety. Her companions detest her, and the nuns, although they admit that she is not exactly naughty, seem to feel her as a dreadful thorn in the flesh. She spends hours and hours on the terrace overlooking the sea (her great desire, she confided to me, is to get to the sea—to get *back to the sea*, as she expressed it), and lying in the garden, under the big myrtle-bushes, and, in spring and summer, under the rose-hedge. The nuns say that rose-hedge and that myrtle-bush are growing a great deal too big, one would think from Dionea's lying under them; the fact, I suppose, has drawn attention to them. "That child makes all the useless weeds grow," remarked Sister Reparata. Another of Dionea's amusements is playing with pigeons. The number of pigeons she collects about her is quite amazing; you would never have thought that San Massimo or the neighbouring hills contained as many. They flutter down like snowflakes, and strut and swell themselves out, and furl and unfurl their tails, and peck with little sharp movements of their silly, sensual heads and a little throb and gurgle in their throats, while Dionea lies stretched out full length in the sun, putting out her lips, which they come to kiss, and uttering strange, cooing sounds; or hopping about, flapping her arms slowly like wings, and raising her little head with much the same odd gesture as they;—'tis a lovely sight, a thing fit for one of your painters, Burne-Jones or Tadema, with the myrtle-bushes all round, the bright, white-washed convent walls behind, the white marble chapel steps (all steps are marble in this Carrara country), and the enamel blue sea through the ilex-branches beyond. But the good Sisters abominate these pigeons, who, it appears, are messy little creatures, and they complain that, were it not that the Reverend Director likes a pigeon in his pot on a holiday, they could not stand the bother of perpetually sweeping the chapel steps and the kitchen threshold all along of those dirty birds. . . .

August 6, 1882.

Do not tempt me, dearest Excellency, with your invitations to Rome. I should not be happy there, and do but little honour to your friendship. My many years of exile, of wanderings in northern countries, have made me a little bit into a northern man: I cannot quite get on with my own fellow-countrymen, except with the good peasants and fishermen all round. Besides—forgive the vanity of an old man, who has learned to make triple acrostic sonnets to cheat the days and months at Theresienstadt and Spielberg—I have suffered too much for Italy to endure patiently the sight of little parliamentary cabals and municipal wranglings, although they also are necessary in this day as conspiracies and battles were in mine. I am not fit for your roomful of ministers and learned men and pretty women: the former would think me an ignoramus, and the latter—what would afflict me much more—a pedant. . . . Rather, if your Excellency really wants to show yourself and your children to your father's old *protégé* of Mazzinian times, find a few days to come here next spring. You shall have some very bare rooms with brick floors and white curtains opening out on my terrace; and a dinner of all manner of fish and milk (the white garlic flowers shall be mown away from under the olives lest my cow should eat it) and eggs cooked in herbs plucked in the hedges. Your boys can go and see the big ironclads at Spezia; and you shall come with me up our lanes fringed with delicate ferns and overhung by big olives, and into the fields where the cherry-trees shed their blossoms on to the budding vines, the fig-trees stretching out their little green gloves, where the goats nibble perched on their hind legs, and the cows low in the huts of reeds; and there rise from the ravines, with the gurgle of the brooks, from the cliffs with the boom of the surf, the voices of unseen boys and girls, singing about love and flowers and death, just as in the days of Theocritus, whom your learned Excellency does well to read. Has your Excellency ever read Longus, a Greek pastoral novelist? He is a trifle free, a trifle nude for us readers of Zola; but the old French of Amyot has a wonderful charm, and he gives one an idea, as no one else does, how folk lived in such valleys, by such sea-boards, as these in the days when daisy-chains and garlands of roses were still hung on the olive-trees for the nymphs of the grove; when across the bay, at the end of the narrow neck of blue sea, there clung to the marble rocks not a church of Saint Laurence, with the sculptured martyr on his gridiron, but the temple of Venus, protecting her harbour. . . . Yes, dear Lady Evelyn, you have guessed aright. Your old friend has returned to his sins, and is scribbling once more. But no longer at verses or political pamphlets. I am enthralled by a tragic history, the history of the fall of the Pagan Gods. . . . Have you ever read of their wanderings and disguises, in my friend Heine's little book?

And if you come to Montemirto, you shall see also your *protégée*, of whom you ask for news. It has just missed being disastrous. Poor Dionea! I fear that early voyage tied to the spar did no good to her wits, poor little waif! There has been a fearful row; and it has required all my influence, and all the awfulness of your Excellency's name, and the Papacy, and the Holy Roman Empire, to prevent her expulsion by the Sisters of the Stigmata. It appears that this mad creature very nearly committed a sacrilege: she was discovered handling in a suspicious manner the Madonna's gala frock and her best veil of *pizzo di Cantù*, a gift of the late Marchioness Violante Vigalena of Fornovo. One of the orphans, Zaira Barsanti, whom they call the Rossaccia, even pretends to have surprised Dionea as she was about to adorn her wicked little person with these sacred garments; and, on another occasion, when Dionea had been sent to pass some oil and sawdust over the chapel floor (it was the eve of Easter of the Roses), to have discovered her seated on the edge of the altar, in the very place of the Most Holy Sacrament. I was sent for in hot haste, and had to assist at an ecclesiastical council in the convent parlour, where Dionea appeared, rather out of place, an amazing little beauty, dark, lithe, with an odd, ferocious gleam in her eyes, and a still odder smile, tortuous, serpentine, like that of Leonardo da Vinci's women, among the plaster images of St. Francis, and the glazed and framed samplers before the little statue of the Virgin, which wears in summer a kind of mosquito-curtain to guard it from the flies, who, as you know, are creatures of Satan.

Speaking of Satan, does your Excellency know that on the inside of our little convent door, just above the little perforated plate of metal (like the rose of a watering-pot) through which the Sister-portress peeps and talks, is pasted a printed form, an arrangement of holy names and texts in triangles, and the stigmatised hands of St. Francis, and a variety of other devices, for the purpose, as is explained in a special notice, of baffling the Evil One, and preventing his entrance into that building? Had you seen Dionea, and the stolid, contemptuous way in which she took, without attempting to refute, the various shocking allegations against her, your Excellency would have reflected, as I did, that the door in question must have been accidentally absent from the premises, perhaps at the joiner's for repair, the day that your *protégée* first penetrated into the convent. The ecclesiastical tribunal, consisting of the Mother Superior, three Sisters, the Capuchin Director, and your humble servant (who vainly attempted to be Devil's advocate), sentenced Dionea, among other things, to make the sign of the cross twenty-six times on the bare floor with her tongue. Poor little child! One might almost expect that, as happened when Dame Venus scratched her hand on the thorn-bush, red roses should sprout up between the fissures of the dirty old bricks.

October 14, 1883.

You ask whether, now that the Sisters let Dionea go and do half a day's service now and then in the village, and that Dionea is a grown-up creature, she does not set the place by the ears with her beauty. The people here are quite aware of its existence. She is already dubbed *La bella Dionea*; but that does not bring her any nearer getting a husband, although your Excellency's generous offer of a wedding-portion is well known throughout the district of San Massimo and Montemirto. None of our boys, peasants or fishermen, seem to hang on her steps; and if they turn round to stare and whisper as she goes by straight and dainty in her wooden clogs, with the pitcher of water or the basket of linen on her beautiful crisp dark head, it is, I remark, with an expression rather of fear than of love. The women, on their side, make horns with their fingers as she passes, and as they sit by her side in the convent chapel; but that seems natural. My housekeeper tells me that down in the village she is regarded as possessing the evil eye and bringing love misery. "You mean," I said, "that a glance from her is too much for our lads' peace of mind." Veneranda shook her head, and explained, with the deference and contempt with which she always mentions any of her countryfolk's superstitions to me, that the matter is different: it's not with her they are in love (they would be afraid of her eye), but where-ever she goes the young people must needs fall in love with each other, and usually where it is far from desirable. "You know Sora Luisa, the blacksmith's widow? Well, Dionea did a *half-service* for her last month, to prepare for the wedding of Luisa's daughter. Well, now, the girl must say, forsooth! that she won't have Pieriho of Lerici any longer, but will have that raggamuffin Wooden Pipe from Solaro, or go into a convent. And the girl changed her mind the very day that Dionea had come into the house. Then there is the wife of Pippo, the coffee-house keeper; they say she is carrying on with one of the coast-guards, and Dionea helped her to do her washing six weeks ago. The son of Sor Temistocle has just cut off a finger to avoid the conscription, because he is mad about his cousin and afraid of being taken for a soldier; and it is a fact that some of the shirts which were made for him at the Stigmata had been sewn by Dionea;" . . . and thus a perfect string of love misfortunes, enough to make a little "Decameron," I assure you, and all laid to Dionea's account. Certain it is that the people of San Massimo are terribly afraid of Dionea. . . .

July 17, 1884.

Dionea's strange influence seems to be extending in a terrible way. I am almost beginning to think that our folk are correct in their fear of the young witch. I used to think, as physician to a convent, that nothing was more erroneous than all the romancings of Diderot and Schubert (your Excellency sang me his "Young Nun" once: do you recollect, just before your marriage?), and that no more humdrum creature existed than one of our little nuns, with their pink baby faces under their tight white caps. It appeared the romancing was more correct than the prose. Unknown things have sprung up in these good Sisters' hearts, as unknown flowers have sprung up among the myrtle-bushes and the rose-hedge which Dionea lies under. Did I ever mention to you a certain little Sister Giuliana, who professed only two years ago?—a funny rose and white little creature presiding over the infirmary, as prosaic a little saint as ever kissed a crucifix or scoured a saucepan. Well, Sister Giuliana has disappeared, and the same day has disappeared also a sailor-boy from the port.

August 20, 1884.

The case of Sister Giuliana seems to have been but the beginning of an extraordinary love epidemic at the Convent of the Stigmata: the elder schoolgirls have to be kept under lock and key lest they should talk over the wall in the moonlight, or steal out to the little hunchback who writes love-letters at a penny a-piece, beautiful flourishes and all, under the portico by the Fish-market. I wonder does that wicked little Dionea, whom no one pays court to, smile (her lips like a Cupid's bow or a tiny snake's curves) as she calls the pigeons down around her, or lies fondling the cats under the myrtle-bush, when she sees the pupils going about with swollen, red eyes; the poor little nuns taking fresh penances on the cold chapel flags; and hears the long-drawn guttural vowels, *amore* and *morte* and *mio bene*, which rise up of an evening, with the boom of the surf and the scent of the lemon-flowers, as the young men wander up and down, arm-in-arm, twanging their guitars along the moonlit lanes under the olives?

October 20, 1885.

A terrible, terrible thing has happened! I write to your Excellency with hands all a-tremble; and yet I *must* write, I must speak, or else I shall cry out. Did I ever mention to you Father Domenico of Casoria, the confessor of our Convent of the Stigmata? A young man, tall, emaciated with fasts and vigils, but handsome like the monk playing the virginal in Giorgione's "Concert," and under his brown serge still the most stalwart fellow of the country all round? One has heard of men struggling with the tempter. Well, well, Father Domenico had struggled as hard as any of the Anchorites recorded by St. Jerome, and he had conquered. I never knew anything comparable to the angelic serenity of gentleness of this victorious soul. I don't like monks, but I loved Father Domenico. I might have been his father, easily, yet I always felt a certain shyness and awe of him; and yet men have accounted me a clean-lived man in my generation; but I felt, whenever I approached him, a poor worldly creature, debased by the knowledge of so many mean and ugly things. Of late Father Domenico had seemed to me less calm than usual: his eyes had grown strangely bright, and red spots had formed on his salient cheekbones. One day last week, taking his hand, I felt his pulse flutter, and all his strength as it were, liquefy under my touch. "You are ill," I said. "You have fever, Father Domenico. You have been overdoing yourself—some new privation, some new penance. Take care and do not tempt Heaven; remember the flesh is weak." Father Domenico withdrew his hand quickly. "Do not say that," he cried; "the flesh is strong!" and turned away his face. His eyes were glistening and he shook all over. "Some quinine," I ordered. But I felt it was no case for quinine. Prayers might be more useful, and could I have given them he should not have wanted. Last night I was suddenly sent for to Father Domenico's monastery above Monte-mirto: they told me he was ill. I ran up through the dim twilight of moonbeams and olives with a sinking heart. Something told me my monk was dead. He was lying in a little low whitewashed room; they had carried him there from his own cell in hopes he might still be alive. The windows were wide open; they framed some olive-branches, glistening in the moonlight, and far below, a strip of moonlit sea. When I told them that he was really dead, they brought some tapers and lit them at his head and feet, and placed a crucifix between his hands. "The Lord has been pleased to call our poor brother to Him," said the Superior. "A case of apoplexy, my dear Doctor—a case of apoplexy. You will make out the certificate for the authorities." I made out the certificate. It was weak of me. But, after all, why make a scandal? He certainly had no wish to injure the poor monks.

Next day I found the little nuns all in tears. They were gathering flowers to send as a last gift to their confessor. In the convent garden I found Dionea, standing by the side of a big basket of roses, one of the white pigeons perched on her shoulder.

"So," she said, "he has killed himself with charcoal, poor Padre Domenico!"

Something in her tone, her eyes, shocked me.

"God has called to Himself one of His most faithful servants," I said gravely.

Standing opposite this girl, magnificent, radiant in her beauty, before the rose-hedge, with the white pigeons furling and unfurling, strutting and pecking all round, I seemed to see suddenly the whitewashed room of last night, the big crucifix, that poor thin face under the yellow waxlight. I felt glad for Father Domenico; his battle was over.

"Take this to Father Domenico from me," said Dionea, breaking off a twig of myrtle starred over with white blossom; and raising her head with that smile like the twist of a young snake, she sang out in a high guttural voice a strange chaunt, consisting of the word *Amor—amor—amor.* I took the branch of myrtle and threw it in her face.

January 3, 1886.

It will be difficult to find a place for Dionea, and in this neighbourhood well-nigh impossible. The people associate her somehow with the death of Father Domenico, which has confirmed her reputation of having the evil eye. She left the convent (being now seventeen) some two months back, and is at present gaining her bread working with the masons at our notary's new house at Lerici: the work is hard, but our women often do it, and it is magnificent to see Dionea, in her short white skirt and tight white bodice, mixing the smoking lime with her beautiful strong arms; or, an empty sack drawn over her head and shoulders, walking majestically up the cliff, up the scaffoldings with her load of bricks. . . . I am, however, very anxious to get Dionea out of the neighbourhood, because I cannot help dreading the annoyances to which her reputation for the evil eye exposes her, and even some explosion of rage if ever she should lose the indifferent contempt with which she treats them. I hear that one of the rich men of our part of the world, a certain Sor Agostino of Sarzana, who owns a whole flank of marble mountain, is looking out for a maid for his daughter, who is about to be married; kind people and patriarchal in their riches, the old man still sitting down to table with all his servants; and his nephew, who is going to be his son-in-law, a splendid young fellow, who has worked like Jacob, in the quarry and at the saw-mill, for love of his pretty cousin. That whole house is so good, simple, and peaceful, that I hope it may tame down even Dionea. If I do not succeed in getting Dionea this place (and all your Excellency's illustriousness and all my poor eloquence will be needed to counteract the sinister reports attaching to our poor little waif), it will be best to accept your suggestion of taking the girl into your household at Rome, since you are curious to see what you call our baleful beauty. I am amused, and a little indignant at what you say about your footmen being handsome: Don Juan himself, my dear Lady Evelyn, would be cowed by Dionea. . . .

May 29, 1886.

Here is Dionea back upon our hands once more! but I cannot send her to your Excellency. Is it from living among these peasants and fishing-folk, or is it

Dionea

because, as people pretend, a sceptic is always superstitious? I could not muster courage to send you Dionea, although your boys are still in sailor-clothes and your uncle, the Cardinal, is eighty-four; and as to the Prince, why, he bears the most potent amulet against Dionea's terrible powers in your own dear capricious person. Seriously, there is something eerie in this coincidence. Poor Dionea! I feel sorry for her, exposed to the passion of a once patriarchally respectable old man. I feel even more abashed at the incredible audacity, I should almost say sacrilegious madness, of the vile old creature. But still the coincidence is strange and uncomfortable. Last week the lightning struck a huge olive in the orchard of Sor Agostino's house above Sarzana. Under the olive was Sor Agostino himself, who was killed on the spot; and opposite, not twenty paces off, drawing water from the well, unhurt and calm, was Dionea. It was the end of a sultry afternoon: I was on a terrace in one of those villages of ours, jammed, like some hardy bush, in the gash of a hillside. I saw the storm rush down the valley, a sudden blackness, and then, like a curse, a flash, a tremendous crash, re-echoed by a dozen hills. "I told him," Dionea said very quietly, when she came to stay with me the next day (for Sor Agostino's family would not have her for another half-minute), "that if he did not leave me alone Heaven would send him an accident."

July 15, 1886.

My book? Oh, dear Donna Evelina, do not make me blush by talking of my book! Do not make an old man, respectable, a Government functionary (communal physician of the district of San Massimo and Montemirto Ligure), confess that he is but a lazy unprofitable dreamer, collecting materials as a child picks hips out of a hedge, only to throw them away, liking them merely for the little occupation of scratching his hands and standing on tiptoe, for their pretty redness. . . . You remember what Balzac says about projecting any piece of work?—*"C'est fumer des cigarettes enchantées."* . . . Well, well! The data obtainable about the ancient gods in their days of adversity are few and far between: a quotation here and there from the Fathers; two or three legends; Venus reappearing; the persecutions of Apollo in Styria; Proserpina going, in Chaucer, to reign over the fairies; a few obscure religious persecutions in the Middle Ages on the score of Paganism; some strange rites practised till lately in the depths of a Breton forest near Lannion. . . . As to Tannhäuser, he was a real knight, and a sorry one, and a real

Minnesinger not of the best. Your Excellency will find some of his poems in Von der Hagen's four immense volumes, but I recommend you to take your notions of Ritter Tannhäuser's poetry rather from Wagner. Certain it is that the Pagan divinities lasted much longer than we suspect, sometimes in their own nakedness, sometimes in the stolen garb of the Madonna or the saints. Who knows whether they do not exist to this day? And, indeed, is it possible they should not? For the awfulness of the deep woods, with their filtered green light, the creak of the swaying, solitary reeds, exists, and is Pan; and the blue, starry May night exists, the sough of the waves, the warm wind carrying the sweetness of the lemon-blossoms, the bitterness of the myrtle on our rocks, the distant chaunt of the boys cleaning out their nets, of the girls sickling the grass under the olives, *Amor—amor—amor*, and all this is the great goddess Venus. And opposite to me, as I write, between the branches of the ilexes, across the blue sea, streaked like a Ravenna mosaic with purple and green, shimmer the white houses and walls, the steeple and towers, an enchanted Fata Morgana city, of dim Porto Venere; . . . and I mumble to myself the verse of Catullus, but addressing a greater and more terrible goddess than he did:—

"Procul a mea sit furor omnis, Hera, domo; alios; age incitatos, alios age rabidos."

March 25, 1887.

Yes; I will do everything in my power for your friends. Are you well-bred folk as well bred as we, Republican *bourgeois*, with the coarse hands (though you once told me mine were psychic hands when the mania of palmistry had not yet been succeeded by that of the Reconciliation between Church and State), I wonder, that you should apologise, you whose father fed me and housed me and clothed me in my exile, for giving me the horrid trouble of hunting for lodgings? It is like you, dear Donna Evelina, to have sent me photographs of my future friend Waldemar's statue. . . . I have no love for modern sculpture, for all the hours I have spent in Gibson's and Dupré's studio: 'tis a dead art we should do better to bury. But your Waldemar has something of the old spirit: he seems to feel the divineness of the mere body, the spirituality of a limpid stream of mere physical life. But why among these statues only men and boys, athletes and fauns? Why only the bust of that thin, delicate-lipped little Madonna wife of his? Why no wide-shouldered Amazon or broad-flanked Aphrodite?

Dionea

April 10, 1887.

You ask me how poor Dionea is getting on. Not as your Excellency and I ought to have expected when we placed her with the good Sisters of the Stigmata: although I wager that, fantastic and capricious as you are, you would be better pleased (hiding it carefully from that grave side of you which bestows devout little books and carbolic acid upon the indigent) that your *protégée* should be a witch than a serving-maid, a maker of philters rather than a knitter of stockings and sewer of shirts.

A maker of philters. Roughly speaking, that is Dionea's profession. She lives upon the money which I dole out to her (with many useless objurgations) on behalf of your Excellency; and her ostensible employment is mending nets, collecting olives, carrying bricks, and other miscellaneous jobs; but her real status is that of village sorceress. You think our peasants are sceptical? Perhaps they do not believe in thought-reading, mesmerism, and ghosts, like you, dear Lady Evelyn. But they believe very firmly in the evil eye, in magic, and in love-potions. Every one has his little story of this or that which happened to his brother or cousin or neighbour. My stable-boy and male factotum's brother-in-law, living some years ago in Corsica, was seized with a longing for a dance with his beloved at one of those balls which our peasants give in the winter, when the snow makes leisure in the mountains. A wizard anointed him for money, and straightway he turned into a black cat, and in three bounds was over the seas, at the door of his uncle's cottage, and among the dancers. He caught his beloved by the skirt to draw her attention; but she replied with a kick which sent him squealing back to Corsica. When he returned in summer he refused to marry the lady, and carried his left arm in a sling. "You broke it when I came to the Veglia!" he said, and all seemed explained. Another lad, returning from working in the vineyards near Marseilles, was walking up to his native village, high in our hills, one moonlight night. He heard sounds of fiddle and fife from a roadside barn, and saw yellow light from its chinks; and then entering, he found many women dancing, old and young, and among them his affianced. He tried to snatch her round the waist for a waltz (they play *Mme. Angot* at our rustic balls), but the girl was unclutchable, and whispered, "Go; for these are witches, who will kill thee; and I am a witch also. Alas! I shall go to hell when I die."

I could tell your Excellency dozens of such stories. But love-philters are among the commonest things to sell and buy. Do you remember the sad little story of Cervantes' Licentiate, who, instead of a love-potion, drank a philter which made him think he was made of glass, fit emblem of a poor mad poet? . . . It is love-philters that Dionea prepares. No; do not misunderstand; they do not give love of her, still less her love. Your seller of love-charms is as cold as ice, as pure as snow. The priest has crusaded against her, and stones have flown at her as she went by from dissatisfied lovers; and the very children, paddling in the sea and making mud-pies in the sand, have put out forefinger and little finger and screamed, "Witch, witch! ugly witch!" as she passed with basket or brick load; but Dionea has only smiled, that snakelike, amused smile, but more ominous than of yore. The other day I determined to seek her and argue with her on the subject of her evil trade. Dionea has a certain regard for me; not, I fancy, a result of gratitude, but rather the recognition of a certain admiration and awe which she inspires in your Excellency's foolish old servant. She has taken up her abode in a deserted hut, built of dried reeds and thatch, such as they keep cows in, among the olives on the cliffs. She was not there, but about the hut pecked some white pigeons, and from it, startling me foolishly with its unexpected sound, came the eerie bleat of her pet goat. . . . Among the olives it was twilight already, with streakings of faded rose in the sky, and faded rose, like long trails of petals, on the distant sea. I clambered down among the myrtle-bushes and came to a little semicircle of yellow sand, between two high and jagged rocks, the place where the sea had deposited Dionea after the wreck. She was seated there on the sand, her bare foot dabbling in the waves; she had twisted a wreath of myrtle and wild roses on her black, crisp hair. Near her was one of our prettiest girls, the Lena of Sor Tullio the blacksmith, with ashy, terrified face under her flowered kerchief. I determined to speak to the child, but without startling her now, for she is a nervous, hysteric little thing. So I sat on the rocks, screened by the myrtle-bushes, waiting till the girl had gone. Dionea, seated listless on the sands, leaned over the sea and took some of its water in the hollow of her hand. "Here," she said to the Lena of Sor Tullio, "fill your bottle with this and give it to drink to Tommasino the Rosebud." Then she set to singing:—

"Love is salt, like sea-water—I drink and I die of thirst. . . . Water! water! Yet the more I drink, the more I burn. Love! thou art bitter as the seaweed."

April 20, 1887.

Your friends are settled here, dear Lady Evelyn. The house is built in what was once a Genoese fort, growing like a grey spiked aloes out of the marble rocks of our bay; rock and wall (the walls existed long before Genoa was ever heard of) grown almost into a homogeneous mass, delicate grey, stained with black and yellow lichen, and dotted here and there with myrtle-shoots and crimson snapdragon. In what was once the highest enclosure of the fort, where your friend Gertrude watches the maids hanging out the fine white sheets and pillow-cases to dry (a bit of the North, of Hermann and Dorothea transferred to the South), a great twisted fig-tree juts out like an eccentric gurgoyle over the sea, and drops its ripe fruit into the deep blue pools. There is but scant furniture in the house, but a great oleander overhangs it, presently to burst into pink splendour; and on all the window-sills, even that of the kitchen (such a background of shining brass saucepans Waldemar's wife has made of it!) are pipkins and tubs full of trailing carnations, and tufts of sweet basil and thyme and mignonette. She pleases me most, your Gertrude, although you foretold I should prefer the husband; with her thin white face, a Memling Madonna finished by some Tuscan sculptor, and her long, delicate white hands ever busy, like those of a mediaeval lady, with some delicate piece of work; and the strange blue, more limpid than the sky and deeper than the sea, of her rarely lifted glance.

It is in her company that I like Waldemar best; I prefer to the genius that infinitely tender and respectful, I would not say *lover*—yet I have no other word—of his pale wife. He seems to me, when with her, like some fierce, generous, wild thing from the woods, like the lion of Una, tame and submissive to this saint. . . . This tenderness is really very beautiful on the part of that big lion Waldemar, with his odd eyes, as of some wild animal—odd, and, your Excellency remarks, not without a gleam of latent ferocity. I think that hereby hangs the explanation of his never doing any but male figures: the female figure, he says (and your Excellency must hold him responsible, not me, for such profanity), is almost inevitably inferior in strength and beauty; woman is not form, but expression, and therefore suits painting, but not sculpture. The point of a woman is not her body, but (and here his eyes rested very tenderly upon the thin white profile of his wife) her soul. "Still," I answered, "the ancients, who understood such matters, did manufacture some tolerable female statues: the Fates of the Parthenon, the Phidian Pallas, the Venus of Milo." . . .

"Ah! yes," exclaimed Waldemar, smiling, with that savage gleam of his eyes; "but those are not women, and the people who made them have left us the tales of Endymion, Adonis, Anchises: a goddess might sit for them." . . .

May 5, 1887.

Has it ever struck your Excellency in one of your La Rochefoucauld fits (in Lent say, after too many balls) that not merely maternal but conjugal unselfishness may be a very selfish thing? There! you toss your little head at my words; yet I wager I have heard you say that *other* women may think it right to humour their husbands, but as to you, the Prince must learn that a wife's duty is as much to chasten her husband's whims as to satisfy them. I really do feel indignant that such a snow-white saint should wish another woman to part with all instincts of modesty merely because that other woman would be a good model for her husband; really it is intolerable. "Leave the girl alone," Waldemar said, laughing. "What do I want with the unæsthetic sex, as Schopenhauer calls it?" But Gertrude has set her heart on his doing a female figure; it seems that folk have twitted him with never having produced one. She has long been on the look-out for a model for him. It is odd to see this pale, demure, diaphanous creature, not the more earthly for approaching motherhood, scanning the girls of our village with the eyes of a slave-dealer.

"If you insist on speaking to Dionea," I said, "I shall insist on speaking to her at the same time, to urge her to refuse your proposal." But Waldemar's pale wife was indifferent to all my speeches about modesty being a poor girl's only dowry. "She will do for a Venus," she merely answered.

We went up to the cliffs together, after some sharp words, Waldemar's wife hanging on my arm as we slowly clambered up the stony path among the olives. We found Dionea at the door of her hut, making faggots of myrtle-branches. She listened sullenly to Gertrude's offer and explanations; indifferently to my admonitions not to accept. The thought of stripping for the view of a man, which would send a shudder through our most brazen village girls, seemed not to startle her, immaculate and savage as she is accounted. She did not answer, but sat under the olives, looking vaguely across the sea. At that moment Waldemar came up to us; he had followed with the intention of putting an end to these wranglings.

"Gertrude," he said, "do leave her alone. I have found a model—a fisher-boy, whom I much prefer to any woman."

Dionea

Dionea raised her head with that serpentine smile. "I will come," she said.

Waldemar stood silent; his eyes were fixed on her, where she stood under the olives, her white shift loose about her splendid throat, her shining feet bare in the grass. Vaguely, as if not knowing what he said, he asked her name. She answered that her name was Dionea; for the rest, she was an Innocentina, that is to say, a foundling; then she began to sing:—

"Flower of the myrtle!
My father is the starry sky;
The mother that made me is the sea."

June 22, 1887.

I confess I was an old fool to have grudged Waldemar his model. As I watch him gradually building up his statue, watch the goddess gradually emerging from the clay heap, I ask myself—and the case might trouble a more subtle moralist than me—whether a village girl, an obscure, useless life within the bounds of what we choose to call right and wrong, can be weighed against the possession by mankind of a great work of art, a Venus immortally beautiful? Still, I am glad that the two alternatives need not be weighed against each other. Nothing can equal the kindness of Gertrude, now that Dionea has consented to sit to her husband; the girl is ostensibly merely a servant like any other; and, lest any report of her real functions should get abroad and discredit her at San Massimo or Montemirto, she is to be taken to Rome, where no one will be the wiser, and where, by the way, your Excellency will have an opportunity of comparing Waldemar's goddess of love with our little orphan of the Convent of the Stigmata. What reassures me still more is the curious attitude of Waldemar towards the girl. I could never have believed that an artist could regard a woman so utterly as a mere inanimate thing, a form to copy, like a tree or flower. Truly he carries out his theory that sculpture knows only the body, and the body scarcely considered as human. The way in which he speaks to Dionea after hours of the most rapt contemplation of her is almost brutal in its coldness. And yet to hear him exclaim, "How beautiful she is! Good God, how beautiful!" No love of mere woman was ever so violent as this love of woman's mere shape.

June 27, 1887.

You asked me once, dearest Excellency, whether there survived among our people (you had evidently added a volume on folk-lore to that heap of half-cut, dog's-eared books that litter about among the Chineseries and mediaeval brocades of your rooms) any trace of Pagan myths. I explained to you then that all our fairy mythology, classic gods, and demons and heroes, teemed with fairies, ogres, and princes. Last night I had a curious proof of this. Going to see the Waldemar, I found Dionea seated under the oleander at the top of the old Genoese fort, telling stories to the two little blonde children who were making the falling pink blossoms into necklaces at her feet; the pigeons, Dionea's white pigeons, which never leave her, strutting and pecking among the basil pots, and the white gulls flying round the rocks overhead. This is what I heard. . . . "And the three fairies said to the youngest son of the King, to the one who had been brought up as a shepherd, 'Take this apple, and give it to her among us who is most beautiful.' And the first fairy said, 'If thou give it to me thou shalt be Emperor of Rome, and have purple clothes, and have a gold crown and gold armour, and horses and courtiers;' and the second said, 'If thou give it to me thou shalt be Pope, and wear a mitre, and have the keys of heaven and hell;' and the third fairy said, 'Give the apple to me, for I will give thee the most beautiful lady to wife.' And the youngest son of the King sat in the green meadow and thought about it a little, and then said, 'What use is there in being Emperor or Pope? Give me the beautiful lady to wife, since I am young myself.' And he gave the apple to the third of the three fairies." . . .

Dionea droned out the story in her half-Genoese dialect, her eyes looking far away across the blue sea, dotted with sails like white sea-gulls, that strange serpentine smile on her lips.

"Who told thee that fable?" I asked.

She took a handful of oleander-blossoms from the ground, and throwing them in the air, answered listlessly, as she watched the little shower of rosy petals descend on her black hair and pale breast—

"Who knows?"

July 6, 1887.

How strange is the power of art! Has Waldemar's statue shown me the real Dionea, or has Dionea really grown more strangely beautiful than before? Your Excellency will laugh; but when I meet her I cast down my eyes after the first glimpse of her loveliness; not with the shyness of a ridiculous old pursuer of the Eternal Feminine, but with a sort of religious awe—the feeling with which, as a child kneeling by my mother's side, I looked down on the church flags when the Mass bell told the elevation of the Host. . . . Do you remember the story of

Zeuxis and the ladies of Crotona, five of the fairest not being too much for his Juno? Do you remember—you, who have read everything—all the bosh of our writers about the Ideal in Art? Why, here is a girl who disproves all this nonsense in a minute; she is far, far more beautiful than Waldemar's statue of her. He said so angrily, only yesterday, when his wife took me into his studio (he has made a studio of the long-desecrated chapel of the old Genoese fort, itself, they say, occupying the site of the temple of Venus).

As he spoke that odd spark of ferocity dilated in his eyes, and seizing the largest of his modelling tools, he obliterated at one swoop the whole exquisite face. Poor Gertrude turned ashy white, and a convulsion passed over her face. . . .

July 15.

I wish I could make Gertrude understand, and yet I could never, never bring myself to say a word. As a matter of fact, what is there to be said? Surely she knows best that her husband will never love any woman but herself. Yet ill, nervous as she is, I quite understand that she must loathe this unceasing talk of Dionea, of the superiority of the model over the statue. Cursed statue! I wish it were finished, or else that it had never been begun.

July 20.

This morning Waldemar came to me. He seemed strangely agitated: I guessed he had something to tell me, and yet I could never ask. Was it cowardice on my part? He sat in my shuttered room, the sunshine making pools on the red bricks and tremulous stars on the ceiling, talking of many things at random, and mechanically turning over the manuscript, the heap of notes of my poor, never-finished book on the Exiled Gods. Then he rose, and walking nervously round my study, talking disconnectedly about his work, his eye suddenly fell upon a little altar, one of my few antiquities, a little block of marble with a carved garland and rams' heads, and a half-effaced inscription dedicating it to Venus, the mother of Love.

"It was found," I explained, "in the ruins of the temple, somewhere on the site of your studio: so, at least, the man said from whom I bought it."

Waldemar looked at it long. "So," he said, "this little cavity was to burn the incense in; or rather, I suppose, since it has two little gutters running into it, for collecting the blood of the victim? Well, well! they were wiser in that day, to wring the neck of a pigeon or burn a pinch of incense than to eat their own hearts out, as we do, all along of Dame Venus;" and he laughed, and left me with that odd ferocious lighting-up of his face. Presently there came a knock at my door. It was Waldemar. "Doctor," he said very quietly, "will you do me a favour? Lend me your little Venus altar—only for a few days, only till the day after to-morrow. I want to copy the design of it for the pedestal of my statue: it is appropriate." I sent the altar to him: the lad who carried it told me that Waldemar had set it up in the studio, and calling for a flask of wine, poured out two glasses. One he had given to my messenger for his pains; of the other he had drunk a mouthful, and thrown the rest over the altar, saying some unknown words. "It must be some German habit," said my servant. What odd fancies this man has!

July 25.

You ask me, dearest Excellency, to send you some sheets of my book: you want to know what I have discovered. Alas! dear Donna Evelina, I have discovered, I fear, that there is nothing to discover; that Apollo was never in Styria; that Chaucer, when he called the Queen of the Fairies Proserpine, meant nothing more than an eighteenth century poet when he called Dolly or Betty Cynthia or Amaryllis; that the lady who damned poor Tannhäuser was not Venus, but a mere little Suabian mountain sprite; in fact, that poetry is only the invention of poets, and that that rogue, Heinrich Heine, is entirely responsible for the existence of *Dieux en Exil*. . . . My poor manuscript can only tell you what St. Augustine, Tertullian, and sundry morose old Bishops thought about the loves of Father Zeus and the miracles of the Lady Isis, none of which is much worth your attention. . . . Reality, my dear Lady Evelyn, is always prosaic: at least when investigated into by bald old gentlemen like me.

And yet, it does not look so. The world, at times, seems to be playing at being poetic, mysterious, full of wonder and romance. I am writing as usual, by my window, the moonlight brighter in its whiteness than my mean little yellow-shining lamp. From the mysterious greyness, the olive groves and lanes beneath my terrace, rises a confused quaver of frogs, and buzz and whirr of insects: something, in sound, like the vague trails of countless stars, the galaxies on galaxies blurred into mere blue shimmer by the moon, which rides slowly across the highest heaven. The olive twigs glisten in the rays: the flowers of the pomegranate and oleander are only veiled as with bluish mist in their scarlet and rose. In the sea is another sea, of molten, rippled silver, or a magic causeway leading to the shining vague offing, the luminous pale sky-line, where the islands of Palmaria and Tino float like unsubstantial, shadowy dolphins.

Dionea

The roofs of Montemirto glimmer among the black, pointing cypresses: farther below, at the end of that half-moon of land, is San Massimo: the Genoese fort inhabited by our friends is profiled black against the sky. All is dark: our fisher-folk go to bed early; Gertrude and the little ones are asleep: they at least are, for I can imagine Gertrude lying awake, the moonbeams on her thin Madonna face, smiling as she thinks of the little ones around her, of the other tiny thing that will soon lie on her breast. . . . There is a light in the old desecrated chapel, the thing that was once the temple of Venus, they say, and is now Waldemar's workshop, its broken roof mended with reeds and thatch. Waldemar has stolen in, no doubt to see his statue again. But he will return, more peaceful for the peacefulness of the night, to his sleeping wife and children. God bless and watch over them! Good-night, dearest Excellency.

July 26.

I have your Excellency's telegram in answer to mine. Many thanks for sending the Prince. I await his coming with feverish longing; it is still something to look forward to. All does not seem over. And yet what can he do?

The children are safe: we fetched them out of their bed and brought them up here. They are still a little shaken by the fire, the bustle, and by finding themselves in a strange house; also, they want to know where their mother is; but they have found a tame cat, and I hear them chirping on the stairs.

It was only the roof of the studio, the reeds and thatch, that burned, and a few old pieces of timber. Waldemar must have set fire to it with great care; he had brought armfuls of faggots of dry myrtle and heather from the bakehouse close by, and thrown into the blaze quantities of pine-cones, and of some resin, I know not what, that smelt like incense. When we made our way, early this morning, through the smouldering studio, we were stifled with a hot church-like perfume: my brain swam, and I suddenly remembered going into St. Peter's on Easter Day as a child.

It happened last night, while I was writing to you. Gertrude had gone to bed, leaving her husband in the studio. About eleven the maids heard him come out and call to Dionea to get up and come and sit to him. He had had this craze once before, of seeing her and his statue by an artificial light: you remember he had theories about the way in which the ancients lit up the statues in their temples. Gertrude, the servants say, was heard creeping downstairs a little later.

Do you see it? I have seen nothing else these

hours, which have seemed weeks and months. He had placed Dionea on the big marble block behind the altar, a great curtain of dull red brocade—you know that Venetian brocade with the gold pomegranate pattern—behind her, like a Madonna of Van Eyck's. He showed her to me once before like this, the whiteness of her neck and breast, the whiteness of the drapery round her flanks, toned to the colour of old marble by the light of the resin burning in pans all round. . . . Before Dionea was the altar—the altar of Venus which he had borrowed from me. He must have collected all the roses about it, and thrown the incense upon the embers when Gertrude suddenly entered. And then, and then . . .

We found her lying across the altar, her pale hair among the ashes of the incense, her blood—she had but little to give, poor white ghost!—trickling among the carved garlands and rams' heads, blackening the heaped-up roses. The body of Waldemar was found at the foot of the castle cliff. Had he hoped, by setting the place on fire, to bury himself among its ruins, or had he not rather wished to complete in this way the sacrifice, to make the whole temple an immense votive pyre? It looked like one, as we hurried down the hills to San Massimo: the whole hillside, dry grass, myrtle, and heather, all burning, the pale short flames waving against the blue moonlit sky, and the old fortress outlined black against the blaze.

August 30.

Of Dionea I can tell you nothing certain. We speak of her as little as we can. Some say they have seen her, on stormy nights, wandering among the cliffs: but a sailor-boy assures me, by all the holy things, that the day after the burning of the Castle Chapel—we never call it anything else—he met at dawn, off the island of Palmaria, beyond the Strait of Porto Venere, a Greek boat, with eyes painted on the prow, going full sail to sea, the men singing as she went. And against the mast, a robe of purple and gold about her, and a myrtle-wreath on her head, leaned Dionea, singing words in an unknown tongue, the white pigeons circling around her.

Jean Lorrain

*Funeral Oration (*Oraison funèbre*)*

I have just buried my friend Jacques. We had been friends since childhood; and we were as close at thirty-four as we had been growing up in the little coastal village, scarcely touched by the torpor and numbing calm of the province, and with our eyes fixed on the eternal dream of the shifting horizons of the moaning seas.

Even here, in Paris, I am haunted by the image of the burial in the village graveyard, all the more desolate in the calm, white, winter landscape; this image pursues me like some obsessive nightmare.

Here, as there, the snowflakes descend like a blanket from a low and leaden sky, and my enduring impression is of nothing more sleep-inducing than this graveyard of quilted corpses, swaddled in white, as though buried in swan's-down.

I see the delicate fretwork of the tomb gates and the dark foliage of the evergreen shrubs, their edges outlined by fine frost. The town is close by but there is no sound, either from workshops, or factory bells;

all the spaces between buildings, all the shouts and murmurs, are stifled by the layers of snow, extinguished by its slow and gentle fall. It is like the cascade of large petals, immaculate and white on the ink-black sea between the high cliffs, immaculately white against the despair of the gloomy sky.

The ceremony is over, and there is a rush of great winter overcoats, dusted with hoar frost, across the cemetery. At the entrance the family stand in line, dressed in black, bare-headed, shivering, while they shake the hands of each guest, puffed up by the condolences; the very image of self-importance.

Jacques' brother has a sickly pallor, intensified by the sickly colour of the sky; it brings to mind the pale faces of Napoleon's frozen troops as they suffered atrocities during the retreat from Moscow.

A moiré silk hat, glossy among the shabby headgear of the locals signals the presence of a Parisian out of place at this pauper's funeral. I recognize de Saunis, a member at Jacques' club, whose path I already crossed on arrival at the railway station.

I go up to him, and we shake hands.

'Have you come from Paris just to attend the ceremony?' I ask.

'Yes, I have,' he replied, and then, ironically, from the depths of his furs, 'I never take the trouble for a wedding, but for a funeral, always.' After a pause, he

Funeral Oration (Oraison funèbre)

continued, 'Poor Armenjean, snuffed out, but he was only thirty-three, wasn't he? What did he die of? Anaemia, perhaps, but more like he was ruined by life – first of all by the parties, and then by ether – that dreadful ether! A pretty habit he acquired from that Suzanne!'

And on that note, the swaggering idiot slips away down a side turning, his back bowed beneath the falling snow, and is off, totally delighted at having spoilt the kindly gesture that brought him here with some silly boulevard gossip: but there are others walking behind us, and he must impress the provincials, and maintain his reputation as a *fin-de-siècle* Parisian, to be a kind of Gaudissart figure by speaking ill of the dead, pursuing his stupid trade as a commercial traveller to the grave.

At the gates of the cemetery, there is another surprise. The door of a coupé bangs open, and Madame ****, a relative of Jacques' – a pretty woman in her thirties, who has been more or less, I believe, his mistress – falls into my arms with stifled sobs, and a histrionic and glamorous show of sorrow, set off by her fresh, rosy complexion, blonde hair, and elegant mourning-dress.

'Such a tragedy, my friend.' (She calls me her friend twice, as if she has known me all her life, and it is the end of the world!) 'I knew he was ill, of course, but how could I foresee this? I have come from Rouen this very morning: I did not receive the telegram until yesterday, I had twenty-five people coming to dinner, and it was impossible to put them off: it was an official dinner! After the soirée, I went to pieces. I felt like an actress who had just lost her mother.'

I look into her eyes, which are very beautiful, dark blue and pearly with tears: she is more of an actress than she believes, this pretty relative, for she did not allow her grief to interfere with one of the few balls of winter. Rouen is thirty leagues away from this provincial hole and her black dress suits her very well: she looks like the actress, Madame Réjane.

But Madame pulls me up into her coupé, all the while dabbing at her eyes with a fine lace handkerchief. 'He loved her so much, that girl, he couldn't live without her, and he died for her as she died.' And clasping me nervously, she said in the unmistakable tones of a jealous woman: 'Was she at least pretty, this Suzanne . . . brunette or blonde . . . because, you know, he has died like her, an etheromaniac, poisoned . . . ?' In telling her what I knew, the secret drama of Jacques' last years suddenly came clear to me. From the few words I had earlier exchanged with de Saunis, and the conversation I

Funeral Oration (Oraison funèbre)

was now having with Madame ****, I began to see a pattern emerge. I saw the disturbing figure of Suzanne Evrard; as a ghoul, or kind of vampire, a phantasmal and tragic being that stands before me a pretty girl, perhaps a little too tall and a little too broad, but with such a shapely figure that she seems like a great, delicious flower, drooping and heavy. I find myself sinisterly dreaming of the peculiar brilliance of her black eyes, the feverish eyes of an etheromaniac, glaring and open against her dull complexion.

Two scenes from the recesses of my memory, which I had hitherto refused to recognize, parade themselves before me, synthesizing for me the image of an evil and deadly spirit.

The first occasion was two years ago. It was the night of the Opera Ball, and Jacques, Suzanne, myself, and a motley crew of male and female partygoers had ended up at the Maison d'Or, until three in the morning . . .

I recall it with the lucidity of a sleepwalker, the remains of the supper, half-finished desserts scattered on the stained tablecloth, the marquise's crystal champagne-glasses still half-full, the women standing before the mirrors, readjusting the hoods of their dominoes upon their foreheads.

Jacques was very drunk, and had fallen asleep, his

forehead resting on his crossed arms on the table. The poor chap was very pale, but he was, nevertheless, very handsome by the light of the flickering candles, which were on the point of burning through to the candlesticks: he was pale, like a corpse, and handsome, but his handsomeness was that of one exhausted by depravity; his thin, red moustache, twisted up at the ends, gave him the look of a swashbuckler.

Suzanne had got up and stood behind him, her full, satin domino making her appear taller than she was. She rested a gloved hand on the sleeper's shoulder in order to rouse him and tell him that it was time to go. 'He's as drunk as a lord!', one of the others giggled; and indeed, Jacques was so drunk that he slumped further forward on the table and made no attempt to get up.

Suzanne took off her gloves then, and laid her bare fingers gently on the nape of his neck, stroking him amorously, and then, scratching him with the tip of her fingernail, she pretended to purr like a cat. Jacques still did not move; desperate times, desperate measures: Suzanne pulled from her domino a gilded bottle stopped with emery, poured some of its contents into a champagne-glass, and brought it to the lips of the sleeper. Jacques awoke with a sudden start. Suzanne, smiling as ever, put the glass into his

Funeral Oration (Oraison funèbre)

hand, whereupon he, suddenly sober, drained it, got up, staggering all the while, put on his fur-trimmed coat, and excused himself. Then we left!

The restorative that Suzanne had administered was none other than ether, that ether which never lets go, and which, six months later – by which time she had earned the reputation of an etheromaniac – was the cause of her death! I see her now, standing majestically in her black domino, pouring poison into her lover with one hand, a hideous and tragic mockery of the gesture just made with her other, which had adjusted her green, satin mask: Suzanne was a woman in a dream that night, masked in pale satin, the colour of which matched her sleeves and the ribbons of her domino.

The second scene from my memory is more recent. Suzanne was already dead, and had been for at least ten months. I am with a crowd of partying night-birds that had ended up at Les Halles, at the Soulas or some similar all-night restaurant.

At the counter were market-gardeners, their scarves tied around their heads, drinking punch or hot toddies, talking in raucous, throaty voices. From a spiral staircase draped in green baize came the strains of a waltz picked out by the finger of a drunk.

In the next room, separated from the counter by

a partition, an amusing scene was taking place. An angry customer, assisted by a policeman and the owner of the establishment, was pulling at the silk sleeves of a young woman.

This creature, an habitué of the all-night restaurant, had come upon the customer in the booth where he was dining; in order to get rid of the sponger, the man – a wholesaler from the provinces – had rummaged in his breast-pocket, and given her twenty sous. Then, when it came for him to pay his bill, he could not find the money; suddenly sobering up, he realized that he was missing twenty francs, and that instead of giving the girl a franc he must have given her a louis.

Incandescent with rage, the man had immediately rushed down to the room below, where the girl was still to be found, stretched out in a dead sleep on a bench. Now, while she doltishly and stubbornly denied the charge, all the while swearing at the owner and laughing at the policeman, she was being stripped and searched.

I can still see the woman's large frame laid out on the bench, with her bare legs dangling from her faded dress, her bonnet over her ear, and her happy, boozy smile (the search had revealed that she had nothing hidden in her black stockings). I can still see her supposed victim, drunk, with staring eyes and

Funeral Oration (Oraison funèbre)

ruffled hair, long strands down over his forehead, his manner desperate but resolute, with a murderous look in his eye. I recall also the shrug of the owner's shoulders as he returned to the counter, and the slouching gait of the policeman as he took up his position once more at the street corner, shrugging like the owner, tired and uncaring.

But that which I remember most of all in the corner of this dive is a very elegant black suit, white cravat, and a sprig of heather in the buttonhole. The man was sat with a bottle of whisky, which he was mixing with ether.

He took a large swig of pure ether, a measure which would have scorched the guts of someone like you and me . . . That etheromaniac, that exhausted night-prowler, that gallivanting party animal, that neurotic who never went to bed before eight o'clock in the morning and never got up until seven in the evening, when the lights came on, that was him, Jacques, my friend from childhood, yesterday's deceased! Four years ago, one of the most celebrated young daddies' boys, had gone from bon viveur to waster . . . What is there to say, he went all out to forget, and he forgot . . .

I saw again the depressed, mute, taciturn figure in the dark corner of Les Halles, his face prematurely aged and sickly, a twenty-nine-year-old man who looked fifty, claimed by ether in the same way as morphine had claimed so many others: Jacques, the lover of that poor Suzanne. Jacques – my friend, Jacques – had become in ten months one of the most charming drunks of our *fin de siècle*.

I find myself now weaving a legend around Jacques' habit, which I would have liked to believe: that he tried to poison the memories of a mistress he worshipped, who had died in the full flush of their relationship, only months into their affair, full of love and sensual intoxication.

But the truth – a sinister and terrifying truth – must be known. Suzanne was an etheromaniac, and they poisoned each other together; killed by her own vice, the woman had bequeathed the same terrible fate to her lover beyond the grave. Jacques had outlived her, but they were complicit in their crime, and so the dead reclaimed the living, and now they are together, for ever.

I have just buried my friend Jacques. We had been friends since childhood; and we were as close at thirty-four as we had been growing up in the little coastal village, scarcely touched by the torpor and numbing calm of the province, and with our eyes fixed on the eternal dream of the shifting horizons of the moaning seas.

Translated by Jane Desmarais, 2011

Ernest Dowson

A Case of Conscience

I

It was in Brittany, and the apples were already acquiring a ruddier, autumnal tint, amid their greens and yellows, though Autumn was not yet; and the country lay very still and fair in the sunset which had befallen, softly and suddenly as is the fashion there. A man and a girl stood looking down in silence at the village, Ploumariel, from their post of vantage, half way up the hill: at its lichened church spire, dotted with little gables, like dove-cotes; at the slated roof of its market; at its quiet white houses. The man's eyes rested on it complacently, with the enjoyment of the painter, finding it charming: the girl's, a little absently, as one who had seen it very often before. She was pretty and very young, but her gray serious eyes, the poise of her head, with its rebellious brown hair braided plainly, gave her a little air of dignity, of reserve which sat piquantly upon her youth. In one ungloved hand, that was brown from the sun, but very beautiful, she held an old parasol, the other played occasionally with a bit of purple heather. Presently she began to speak, using English just coloured by a foreign accent, that made her speech prettier.

'You make me afraid,' she said, turning her large, troubled eyes on her companion, 'you make me afraid, of myself chiefly, but a little of you. You suggest so much to me that is new, strange, terrible. When you speak, I am troubled; all my old landmarks appear to vanish; I even hardly know right from wrong. I love you, my God, how I love you! but I want to go away from you and pray in the little quiet church, where I made my first Communion. I will come to the world's end with you; but oh, Sebastian, do not ask me, let me go. You will forget me, I am a little girl to you, Sebastian. You cannot care very much for me.'

The man looked down at her, smiling masterfully, but very kindly. He took the mutinous hand, with its little sprig of heather, and held it between his own. He seemed to find her insistence adorable; mentally, he was contrasting her with all other women whom he had known, frowning at the memory of so many years in which she had no part. He was a man of more than forty, built large to an uniform English pattern; there was a touch of military erectness in his carriage which often deceived people as to his vocation. Actually, he had never been anything but artist, though he came of a family of soldiers, and had once been war correspondent of an illustrated paper. A certain distinction had always adhered to him, never more than now when he was no longer young, was growing bald, had streaks of gray in his moustache. His face, without being handsome, possessed a certain charm; it was worn and rather pale, the lines about the firm mouth were full of lassitude, the eyes rather tired. He had the air of having tasted widely, curiously, of life in his day, prosperous as he seemed now, that had left its mark upon him. His voice, which usually took an intonation that his friends found supercilious, grew very tender in addressing this little French girl, with her quaint air of childish dignity.

'Marie-Yvonne, foolish child, I will not hear one word more. You are a little heretic; and I am sorely tempted to seal your lips from uttering heresy. You tell me that you love me, and you ask me to let you go, in one breath. The impossible conjuncture! Marie-Yvonne,' he added, more seriously, 'trust yourself to me, my child! You know, I will never give you up. You know that these months that I have been at Ploumariel, are worth all the rest of my life to me. It has been a difficult life, hitherto, little one: change it for me; make it worth while. You would let morbid fancies come between us. You have lived overmuch in that little church, with its worm-eaten benches, and its mildewed odour of dead people, and dead ideas. Take care, Marie-Yvonne: it has made you serious-eyed, before you have learnt to laugh; by and by, it will steal away your youth, before you have ever been young. I come to claim you, Marie-Yvonne, in the name of Life.' His words were half-jesting; his eyes were profoundly in earnest. He drew her to him gently; and when he bent down and kissed her forehead, and then her shy lips, she made no resistance: only, a little tremor ran through her. Presently, with equal gentleness, he put her away from him. 'You have already given me your answer, Marie-Yvonne. Believe me, you will never regret it. Let us go down.'

They took their way in silence towards the village; presently a bend of the road hid them from it, and he drew closer to her, helping her with his arm over the rough stones. Emerging, they had gone thirty yards so, before the scent of English tobacco drew their attention to a figure seated by the roadside, under a hedge; they recognised it, and started apart, a little consciously.

'It is M. Tregellan,' said the young girl, flushing: 'and he must have seen us.'

A Case of Conscience

Her companion, frowning, hardly suppressed a little quick objurgation.

'It makes no matter,' he observed, after a moment: 'I shall see your uncle to-morrow and we know, good man, how he wishes this; and, in any case, I would have told Tregellan.'

The figure rose, as they drew near: he shook the ashes out of his briar, and removed it to his pocket. He was a slight man, with an ugly, clever face; his voice as he greeted them, was very low and pleasant.

'You must have had a charming walk, Mademoiselle. I have seldom seen Ploumariel look better.'

'Yes,' she said, gravely, 'it has been very pleasant. But I must not linger now,' she added breaking a little silence in which none of them seemed quite at ease. 'My uncle will be expecting me to supper.' She held out her hand, in the English fashion, to Tregellan, and then to Sebastian Murch; who gave the little fingers a private pressure.

They had come into the market-place round which most of the houses in Ploumariel were grouped. They watched the young girl cross it briskly; saw her blue gown pass out of sight down a bye street: then they turned to their own hotel. It was a low, white house, belted half way down the front with black stone; a pictorial object, as most

Breton hostels. The ground floor was a *café*; and, outside it, a bench and long stained table enticed them to rest. They sat down, and ordered *absinthes*, as the hour suggested: these were brought to them presently by an old servant of the house; an admirable figure, with the white sleeves and apron relieving her linsey dress: with her good Breton face, and its effective wrinkles. For some time they sat in silence, drinking and smoking. The artist appeared to be absorbed in contemplation of his drink; considering its clouded green in various lights. After a while the other looked up, and remarked, abruptly.

'I may as well tell you that I happened to overlook you, just now, unintentionally.'

Sebastian Murch held up his glass, with absent eyes.

'Don't mention it, my dear fellow,' he remarked, at last, urbanely.

'I beg your pardon; but I am afraid I must.'

He spoke with an extreme deliberation which suggested nervousness; with the air of a person reciting a little set speech, learnt imperfectly: and he looked very straight in front of him, out into the street, at two dogs quarrelling over some offal.

'I daresay you will be angry: I can't avoid that; at least, I have known you long enough to hazard it. I have had it on my mind to say something. If I have been silent, it hasn't been because I have been blind, or approved. I have seen how it was all along. I gathered it from your letters when I was in England. Only until this afternoon I did not know how far it had gone, and now I am sorry I did not speak before.'

He stopped short, as though he expected his friend's subtilty to come to his assistance; with admissions or recriminations. But the other was still silent, absent: his face wore a look of annoyed indifference. After a while, as Tregellan still halted, he observed quietly:

'You must be a little more explicit. I confess I miss your meaning.'

'Ah, don't be paltry,' cried the other, quickly. 'You know my meaning. To be very plain, Sebastian, are you quite justified in playing with that charming girl, in compromising her?'

The artist looked up at last, smiling; his expressive mouth was set, not angrily, but with singular determination.

'With Mademoiselle Mitouard?'

'Exactly; with the niece of a man whose guest you have recently been.'

'My dear fellow!' he stopped a little, considering his words: 'You are hasty and uncharitable for such a very moral person! you jump at conclusions,

Tregellan. I don't, you know, admit your right to question me: still, as you have introduced the subject, I may as well satisfy you. I have asked Mademoiselle Mitouard to marry me, and she has consented, subject to her uncle's approval. And that her uncle, who happens to prefer the English method of courtship, is not likely to refuse.'

The other held his cigar between two fingers, a little away; his curiously anxious face suggested that the question had become to him one of increased nicety.

'I am sorry,' he said, after a moment; 'this is worse than I imagined; it's impossible.'

'It is you that are impossible, Tregellan,' said Sebastian Murch. He looked at him now, quite frankly, absolutely: his eyes had a defiant light in them, as though he hoped to be criticised; wished nothing better than to stand on his defence, to argue the thing out. And Tregellan sat for a long time without speaking, appreciating his purpose. It seemed more monstrous the closer he considered it: natural enough withal, and so, harder to defeat; and yet, he was sure, that defeated it must be. He reflected how accidental it had all been: their presence there, in Ploumariel, and the rest! Touring in Brittany, as they had often done before, in their habit of old friends, they had fallen upon it by chance, a place unknown of Murray; and the merest chance had held them there. They had slept at the *Lion d'Or*, voted it magnificently picturesque, and would have gone away and forgotten it; but the chance of travel had for once defeated them. Hard by they heard of the little votive chapel of Saint Bernard; at the suggestion of their hostess they set off to visit it. It was built steeply on an edge of rock, amongst odorous pines overhanging a ravine, at the bottom of which they could discern a brown torrent purling tumidly along. For the convenience of devotees, iron rings, at short intervals, were driven into the wall; holding desperately to these, the pious pilgrim, at some peril, might compass the circuit; saying an oraison to Saint Bernard, and some ten *Aves*. Sebastian, who was charmed with the wild beauty of the scene, in a country ordinarily so placid, had been seized with a fit of emulation: not in any mood of devotion, but for the sake of a wider prospect. Tregellan had protested: and the Saint, resenting the purely æsthetic motive of the feat, had seemed to intervene. For, half-way round, growing giddy may be, the artist had made a false step, lost his hold. Tregellan, with a little cry of horror, saw him disappear amidst crumbling mortar and uprooted ferns. It was with a sensible relief, for the fall had the illusion of great depth, that, making his way rapidly down a winding path, he found him lying on a grass terrace, amidst *débris* twenty feet lower, cursing his folly, and holding a lamentably sprained ankle, but for the rest uninjured! Tregellan had made off in haste to Ploumariel in search of assistance; and within the hour he had returned with two stalwart Bretons and M. le Docteur Mitouard.

Their tour had been, naturally, drawing to its close. Tregellan indeed had an imperative need to be in London within the week. It seemed, therefore, a clear dispensation of Providence, that the amiable doctor should prove an hospitable person, and one inspiring confidence no less. Caring greatly for things foreign, and with an especial passion for England, a country whence his brother had brought back a wife; M. le Docteur Mitouard insisted that the invalid could be cared for properly at his house alone. And there, in spite of protestations, earnest from Sebastian, from Tregellan half-hearted, he was installed. And there, two days later, Tregellan left him with an easy mind; bearing away with him, half enviously, the recollection of the young, charming face of a girl, the Doctor's niece, as he had seen her standing by his friend's sofa when he paid his *adieux*; in the beginnings of an intimacy, in which, as he foresaw, the petulance of the invalid, his impatience at an enforced detention, might be considerably forgot. And all that had been two months ago.

II

'I am sorry you don't see it,' continued Tregellan, after a pause, 'to me it seems impossible; considering your history it takes me by surprise.'

The other frowned slightly; finding this persistence perhaps a trifle crude, he remarked good-humouredly enough:

'Will you be good enough to explain your opposition? Do you object to the girl? You have been back a week now, during which you have seen almost as much of her as I.'

'She is a child, to begin with; there is five-and-twenty years' disparity between you. But it's the relation I object to, not the girl. Do you intend to live in Ploumariel?'

Sebastian smiled, with a suggestion of irony.

'Not precisely; I think it would interfere a little with my career; why do you ask?'

'I imagined not; you will go back to London with your little Breton wife, who is as charming here as the apple-blossom in her own garden. You will introduce her to your circle, who will receive her with open arms; all the clever bores, who write, and talk, and paint, and are talked about between Bloomsbury and Kensington. Everybody who is emancipated will know her, and everybody who has a "fad"; and they will come in a body and emancipate her, and teach her their "fads."'

'That is a caricature of my circle, as you call it, Tregellan! though I may remind you it is also yours. I think she is being starved in this corner, spiritually. She has a beautiful soul, and it has had no chance. I propose to give it one, and I am not afraid of the result.'

Tregellan threw away the stump of his cigar into the darkling street, with a little gesture of discouragement, of lassitude.

'She has had the chance to become what she is, a perfect thing.'

'My dear fellow,' exclaimed his friend, 'I could not have said more myself.'

The other continued, ignoring his interruption.

'She has had great luck. She has been brought up by an old eccentric, on the English system of growing up as she liked. And no harm has come of it, at least until it gave you the occasion of making love to her.'

'You are candid, Tregellan!'

'Let her go, Sebastian, let her go,' he continued, with increasing gravity. 'Consider what a transplantation; from this world of Ploumariel where everything is fixed for her by that venerable old *Curé*, where life is so easy, so ordered, to yours, ours; a world without definitions, where everything is an open question.'

'Exactly,' said the artist, 'why should she be so limited? I would give her scope, ideas. I can't see that I am wrong.'

'She will not accept them, your ideas. They will trouble her, terrify her; in the end, divide you. It is not an elastic nature. I have watched it.'

'At least, allow me to know her,' put in the artist, a little grimly.

Tregellan shook his head.

'The Breton blood; her English mother: passionate Catholicism! a touch of Puritan! Have you quite made up your mind, Sebastian?'

'I made it up long ago, Tregellan!'

The other looked at him, curiously, compassionately; with a touch of resentment at what he found his lack of subtlety. Then he said at last:

'I called it impossible: you force me to be very explicit, even cruel. I must remind you, that you are, of all my friends, the one I value most, could least afford to lose.'

'You must be going to say something extremely disagreeable! something horrible,' said the artist, slowly.

'I am,' said Tregellan, 'but I must say it. Have you explained to Mademoiselle, or her uncle, your—your peculiar position?'

Sebastian was silent for a moment, frowning: the lines about his mouth grew a little sterner; at last he said coldly:

'If I were to answer, Yes?'

'Then I should understand that there was no further question of your marriage.'

Presently the other commenced in a hard, leaden voice.

'No, I have not told Marie-Yvonne that. I shall not tell her. I have suffered enough for a youthful folly; an act of mad generosity. I refuse to allow an infamous woman to wreck my future life as she has disgraced my past. Legally, she has passed out of it; morally, legally, she is not my wife. For all I know she may be actually dead.'

The other was watching his face, very gray and old now, with an anxious compassion.

'You know she is not dead, Sebastian,' he said simply. Then he added very quietly as one breaks supreme bad tidings, 'I must tell you something which I fear you have not realised. The Catholic Church does not recognise divorce. If she marry you and find out, rightly or wrongly she will believe that she has been living in sin; some day she will find it out. No damnable secret like that keeps itself for ever: an old newspaper, a chance remark from one of your dear friends, and, the deluge. Do you see the tragedy, the misery of it? By God, Sebastian, to save you both somebody shall tell her; and if it be not you, it must be I.'

There was extremest peace in the quiet square; the houses seemed sleepy at last, after a day of exhausting tranquillity, and the chestnuts, under which a few children, with tangled hair and fair dirty faces, still played. The last glow of the sun fell on the gray roofs opposite; dying hard it seemed over the street in which the Mitouards lived; and they heard suddenly the tinkle of an *Angelus* bell. Very placid! the place and the few peasants in their pictorial hats and caps who lingered. Only the two Englishmen sitting, their glasses empty, and their smoking over, looking out on it all with their anxious faces, brought in a contrasting note of modern life; of the complex aching life of cities, with its troubles and its difficulties.

'Is that your final word, Tregellan?' asked the artist at last, a little wearily.

'It must be, Sebastian! Believe me, I am infinitely sorry.'

'Yes, of course,' he answered quickly, acidly; 'well, I will sleep on it.'

III

They made their first breakfast in an almost total silence; both wore the bruised harassed air which tells of a night passed without benefit of sleep. Immediately afterwards Murch went out alone: Tregellan could guess the direction of his visit, but not its object; he wondered if the artist was making his difficult confession. Presently they brought him in a pencilled note; he recognised, with some surprise, his friend's tortuous hand.

'I have considered our conversation, and your unjustifiable interference. I am entirely in your hands: at the mercy of your extraordinary notions of duty. Tell her what you will, if you must; and pave the way to your own success. I shall say nothing; but I swear you love the girl yourself; and are no right arbiter here, Sebastian Murch.'

He read the note through twice before he grasped its purport; then sat holding it in lax fingers, his face grown singularly gray.

'It's not true, it's not true,' he cried aloud, but a moment later knew himself for a self-deceiver all along. Never had self-consciousness been more sudden, unexpected, or complete. There was no more to do or say; this knowledge tied his hands. *Ite! missa est!* . . .

A Case of Conscience

He spent an hour painfully invoking casuistry, tossed to and fro irresolutely, but never for a moment disputing that plain fact which Sebastian had so brutally illuminated. Yes! he loved her, had loved her all along. Marie-Yvonne! how the name expressed her! at once sweet and serious, arch and sad as her nature. The little Breton wild flower! how cruel it seemed to gather her! And he could do no more; Sebastian had tied his hands. Things must be! He was a man nicely conscientious, and now all the elaborate devices of his honour, which had persuaded him to a disagreeable interference, were contraposed against him. This suspicion of an ulterior motive had altered it, and so at last he was left to decide with a sigh, that because he loved these two so well, he must let them go their own way to misery.

Coming in later in the day, Sebastian Murch found his friend packing.

'I have come to get your answer,' he said; 'I have been walking about the hills like a madman for hours. I have not been near her; I am afraid. Tell me what you mean to do?'

Tregellan rose, shrugged his shoulders, pointed to his valise.

'God help you both! I would have saved you if you had let me. The Quimperlé *Courrier* passes in half-an-hour. I am going by it. I shall catch a night train to Paris.'

As Sebastian said nothing; continued to regard him with the same dull, anxious gaze, he went on after a moment:

'You did me a grave injustice; you should have known me better than that. God knows I meant nothing shameful, only the best; the least misery for you and her.'

'It was true then?' said Sebastian, curiously. His voice was very cold; Tregellan found him altered. He regarded the thing as it had been very remote, and outside them both.

'I did not know it then,' said Tregellan, shortly.

He knelt down again and resumed his packing. Sebastian, leaning against the bed, watched him with absent intensity, which was yet alive to trivial things, and he handed him from time to time a book, a brush, which the other packed mechanically with elaborate care. There was no more to say, and presently, when the chambermaid entered for his luggage, they went down and out into the splendid sunshine, silently. They had to cross the Square to reach the carriage, a dusty ancient vehicle, hooded, with places for four, which waited outside the post-office. A man in a blue blouse preceded them, carrying Tregellan's things. From the corner they could look down the road to Quimperlé, and their eyes both sought the white house of Doctor Mitouard, standing back a little in its trim garden, with its one incongruous apple tree; but there was no one visible.

Presently, Sebastian asked, suddenly:

'Is it true, that you said last night: divorce to a Catholic—?'

Tregellan interrupted him.

'It is absolutely true, my poor friend.'

He had climbed into his place at the back, settled himself on the shiny leather cushion: he appeared to be the only passenger. Sebastian stood looking drearily in at the window, the glass of which had long perished.

'I wish I had never known, Tregellan! How could I ever tell her!'

Inside, Tregellan shrugged his shoulders: not impatiently, or angrily, but in sheer impotence; as one who gave it up.

'I can't help you,' he said, 'you must arrange it with your own conscience.'

'Ah, it's too difficult!' cried the other: 'I can't find my way.'

The driver cracked his whip, suggestively; Sebastian drew back a little further from the off wheel.

'Well,' said the other, 'if you find it, write and tell me. I am very sorry, Sebastian.'

'Good-bye,' he replied. 'Yes! I will write.'

The carriage lumbered off, with a lurch to the right, as it turned the corner; it rattled down the hill, raising a cloud of white dust. As it passed the Mitouards' house, a young girl, in a large straw hat, came down the garden; too late to discover whom it contained. She watched it out of sight, indifferently, leaning on the little iron gate; then she turned, to recognise the long stooping figure of Sebastian Murch, who advanced to meet her.

NETTA SYRETT

Thy Heart's Desire

I

The tents were pitched in a little plain surrounded by hills. Right and left there were stretches of tender vivid green where the young corn was springing; further still, on either hand, the plain was yellow with mustard-flower; but in the immediate foreground it was bare and stony. A few thorny bushes pushed their straggling way through the dry soil, ineffectively as far as the grace of the landscape was concerned, for they merely served to emphasise the barren aridness of the land that stretched before the tents, sloping gradually to the distant hills.

The hills were uninteresting enough in themselves; they had no grandeur of outline, no picturesqueness even, though at morning and evening the sun, like a great magician, clothed them with beauty at a touch.

They had begun to change, to soften, to blush rose-red in the evening light, when a woman came to the entrance of the largest of the tents and looked towards them. She leant against the support on one side of the canvas flap, and putting back her head, rested that too against it, while her eyes wandered over the plain and over the distant hills.

She was bareheaded, for the covering of the tent projected a few feet to form an awning overhead. The gentle breeze which had risen with sundown, stirred the soft brown tendrils of hair on her temples, and fluttered her pink cotton gown a little. She stood very still, with her arms hanging and her hands clasped loosely in front of her. There was about her whole attitude an air of studied quiet which in some vague fashion the slight clasp of her hands accentuated. Her face, with its tightly, almost rigidly closed lips, would have been quite in keeping with the impression of conscious calm which her entire presence suggested, had it not been that when she raised her eyes a strange contradiction to this idea was afforded. They were large grey eyes, unusually bright and rather startling in effect, for they seemed the only live thing about her. Gleaming from her still set face, there was something almost alarming in their brilliancy. They softened with a sudden glow of pleasure as they rested on the translucent green of the wheat fields under the broad generous sunlight, and then wandered to where the pure vivid yellow of the mustard-flower spread in waves to the base of the hills, now mystically veiled in radiance. She stood motionless watching their melting elusive changes from palpitating rose to the transparent purple of amethyst. The stillness of evening was broken by the monotonous, not unmusical creaking of a Persian wheel at some little distance to the left of the tent. The well stood in a little grove of trees: between their branches she could see, when she turned her head, the coloured *saris* of the village women, where they stood in groups chattering as they drew the water, and the little naked brown babies that toddled beside them or sprawled on the hard ground beneath the trees. From the village of flat-roofed mud-houses under the low hill at the back of the tents, other women were crossing the plain towards the well, their terra-cotta water-jars poised easily on their heads, casting long shadows on the sunbaked ground as they came.

Presently, in the distance, from the direction of the sunlit hills opposite, a little group of men came into sight. Far off, the mustard-coloured jackets and the red turbans of the orderlies made vivid splashes of colour on the dull plain. As they came nearer, the guns slung across their shoulders, the cases of mathematical instruments, the hammers and other heavy baggage they carried for the Sahib, became visible.

A little in front, at walking pace, rode the Sahib himself, making notes as he came in a book he held before him. The girl at the tent-entrance watched the advance of the little company indifferently, it seemed; except for a slight tightening of the muscles about her mouth, her face remained unchanged. While he was still some little distance away, the man with the note-book raised his head and smiled awkwardly as he saw her standing there. Awkwardness, perhaps, best describes the whole man. He was badly put together, loose-jointed, ungainly. The fact that he was tall profited him nothing, for it merely emphasised the extreme ungracefulness of his figure. His long pale face was made paler by a shock of coarse, tow-coloured hair; his eyes even looked colourless, though they were certainly the least uninteresting feature of his face, for they were not devoid of expression. He had a way of slouching when he moved that singularly intensified the general uncouthness of his appearance. "Are you very tired?" asked his wife gently when he had dismounted close to the tent. The question would have been an unnecessary one had it been put to her instead of to her husband, for her voice had that peculiar flat toneless sound for which extreme weariness is answerable.

"Well, no, my dear, not very," he replied,

drawling out the words with an exasperating air of delivering a final verdict, after deep reflection on the subject.

The girl glanced once more at the fading colours on the hills. "Come in and rest," she said, moving aside a little to let him pass.

She stood lingering a moment after he had entered the tent, as though unwilling to leave the outer air; and before she turned to follow him she drew a deep breath, and her hand went for one swift second to her throat as though she felt stifled.

Later on that evening she sat in her tent sewing by the light of the lamp that stood on her little table.

Opposite to her, her husband stretched his ungainly length in a deck-chair, and turned over a pile of official notes. Every now and then her eyes wandered from the gay silks of the table-cover she was embroidering to the canvas walls which bounded the narrow space into which their few household goods were crowded. Outside there was a deep hush. The silence of the vast empty plain seemed to work its way slowly, steadily in, towards the little patch of light set in its midst. The girl felt it in every nerve; it was as though some soft-footed, noiseless, shapeless creature, whose presence she only dimly divined, was approaching nearer—*nearer*.

The heavy outer stillness was in some way made more terrifying by the rustle of the papers her husband was reading, by the creaking of his chair as he moved, and by the little fidgeting grunts and half exclamations which from time to time broke from him. His wife's hand shook at every unintelligible mutter from him, and the slight habitual contraction between her eyes deepened.

All at once she threw her work down on to the table. "For Heaven's sake—*please*, John, *talk!*" she cried. Her eyes, for the moment's space in which they met the startled ones of her husband, had a wild hunted look, but it was gone almost before his slow brain had time to note that it had been there—and was vaguely disturbing. She laughed a little, unsteadily.

"Did I startle you? I'm sorry. I—" she laughed again. "I believe I'm a little nervous. When one is all day alone—" She paused without finishing the sentence. The man's face changed suddenly. A wave of tenderness swept over it, and at the same time an expression of half-incredulous delight shone in his pale eyes.

"Poor little girl, are you really lonely?" he said. Even the real feeling in his tone failed to rob his voice of its peculiarly irritating grating quality. He rose awkwardly and moved to his wife's side.

Involuntarily she shrank a little, and the hand which he had stretched out to touch her hair sank to his side. She recovered herself immediately and turned her face up to his, though she did not raise her eyes; but he did not kiss her. Instead, he stood in an embarrassed fashion a moment by her side, and then went back to his seat.

There was silence again for some time. The man lay back in his chair, gazing at his big clumsy shoes, as though he hoped for some inspiration from that quarter, while his wife worked with nervous haste.

"Don't let me keep you from reading, John," she said, and her voice had regained its usual gentle tone.

"No, my dear; I'm just thinking of something to say to you, but I don't seem—"

She smiled a little. In spite of herself, her lip curled faintly. "Don't worry about it—it was stupid of me to expect it. I mean—" she added hastily, immediately repenting the sarcasm. She glanced furtively at him, but his face was quite unmoved. Evidently he had not noticed it, and she smiled faintly again.

"Oh, Kathie, I knew there was *something* I'd forgotten to tell you, my dear; there's a man coming down here. I don't know whether—"

She looked up sharply. "A man coming *here?* What for?" she interrupted breathlessly.

"Sent to help me about this oil-boring business, my dear."

He had lighted his pipe, and was smoking placidly, taking long whiffs between his words.

"Well?" impatiently questioned his wife, fixing her bright eyes on his face.

"Well—that's all, my dear."

She checked an exclamation. "But don't you know anything about him—his name? where he comes from? what he is like?" She was leaning forward against the table, her needle with a long end of yellow silk drawn halfway through her work, held in her upraised hand, her whole attitude one of quivering excitement and expectancy.

The man took his pipe from his mouth deliberately, with a look of slow wonder.

"Why Kathie, you seem quite anxious. I didn't know you'd be so interested, my dear. Well,"—another long pull at his pipe—"his name's Brook—*Brookfield*, I think." He paused again. "This pipe don't draw well a bit; there's something wrong with it, I shouldn't wonder," he added, taking it out and examining the bowl as though struck with the brilliance of the idea.

Thy Heart's Desire

The woman opposite put down her work and clenched her hands under the table.

"Go on, John," she said presently in a tense vibrating voice—"his name is Brookfield. Well, where does he come from?"

"Straight from home, my dear, I believe." He fumbled in his pocket, and after some time extricated a pencil with which he began to poke the tobacco in the bowl in an ineffectual aimless fashion, becoming completely engrossed in the occupation apparently. There was another long pause. The woman went on working, or feigning to work, for her hands were trembling a good deal.

After some moments she raised her head again. "John, will you mind attending to me one moment, and answering these questions as quickly as you can?" The emphasis on the last word was so faint as to be almost as imperceptible as the touch of exasperated contempt which she could not absolutely banish from her tone.

Her husband, looking up, met her clear bright gaze and reddened like a schoolboy.

"Whereabouts '*from home*' does he come?" she asked in a studiedly gentle fashion.

"Well, from London, I think," he replied, almost briskly for him, though he stammered and tripped over the words. "He's a University chap; I used to hear he was clever—I don't know about that, I'm sure; he used to chaff me, I remember, but—"

"Chaff *you?* You have met him then?"

"Yes, my dear"—he was fast relapsing into his slow drawl again—"that is, I went to school with him, but it's a long time ago. Brookfield—yes, that must be his name."

She waited a moment, then "When is he coming?" she inquired abruptly.

"Let me see—to-day's—"

"*Monday*," the word came swiftly between her set teeth.

"Ah, yes,—Monday—well," reflectively, "*next* Monday, my dear."

Mrs. Drayton rose, and began to pace softly the narrow passage between the table and the tent-wall, her hands clasped loosely behind her.

"How long have you known this?" she said, stopping abruptly. "Oh, John, you *needn't* consider; it's quite a simple question. To-day? Yesterday?"

Her foot moved restlessly on the ground as she waited.

"I think it was the day before yesterday," he replied.

"Then why in Heaven's name didn't you tell me before?" she broke out fiercely.

"My dear, it slipped my memory. If I'd thought you would be interested—"

"Interested!" She laughed shortly. "It *is* rather interesting to hear that after six months of this"—she made a quick comprehensive gesture with her hand—"one will have some one to speak to—some one. It is the hand of Providence; it comes just in time to save me from—" She checked herself abruptly.

He sat staring up at her stupidly, without a word.

"It's all right, John," she said, with a quick change of tone, gathering up her work quietly as she spoke. "I'm not mad—yet. You—you must get used to these little outbreaks," she added after a moment, smiling faintly, "and to do me justice, I don't *often* trouble you with them, do I? I'm just a little tired, or it's the heat or—something. No—don't touch me," she cried, shrinking back, for he had risen slowly and was coming towards her.

She had lost command over her voice, and the shrill note of horror in it was unmistakable. The man heard it, and shrank in his turn.

"I'm so sorry, John," she murmured, raising her great bright eyes to his face. They had not lost their goaded expression, though they were full of tears.

"I'm awfully sorry, but I'm just nervous and stupid, and I can't bear *any one* to touch me when I'm nervous."

II

"Here's Broomhurst, my dear! I made a mistake in his name after all, I find. I told you *Brookfield*, I believe, didn't I? Well, it isn't Brookfield, he says; it's Broomhurst."

Mrs. Drayton had walked some little distance across the plain to meet and welcome the expected guest. She stood quietly waiting while her husband stammered over his incoherent sentences, and then put out her hand.

"We are very glad to see you," she said with a quick glance at the newcomer's face as she spoke.

As they walked together towards the tent, after the first greetings, she felt his keen eyes upon her before he turned to her husband.

"I'm afraid Mrs. Drayton finds the climate trying?" he asked. "Perhaps she ought not to have come so far in this heat?"

"Kathie is often pale. You *do* look white to-day, my dear," he observed, turning anxiously towards his wife.

"Do I?" she replied. The unsteadiness of her tone was hardly appreciable, but it was not lost on

Broomhurst's quick ears. "Oh, I don't think so. I *feel* very well."

"I'll come and see if they've fixed you up all right," said Drayton, following his companion towards the new tent that had been pitched at some little distance from the large one.

"We shall see you at dinner then?" Mrs. Drayton observed in reply to Broomhurst's smile as they parted.

She entered the tent slowly, and moving up to the table, already laid for dinner, began to rearrange the things upon it in a purposeless mechanical fashion.

After a moment she sank down upon a seat opposite the open entrance, and put her hand to her head.

"What is the matter with me?" she thought wearily. "All the week I've been looking forward to seeing this man—*any* man, *any one* to take off the edge of this." She shuddered. Even in thought she hesitated to analyse the feeling that possessed her. "Well, he's here, and I think I feel *worse*." Her eyes travelled towards the hills she had been used to watch at this hour, and rested on them with a vague unseeing gaze.

"Tired, Kathie? A penny for your thoughts, my dear," said her husband, coming in presently to find her still sitting there.

"I'm thinking what a curious world this is, and what an ironical vein of humour the gods who look after it must possess," she replied with a mirthless laugh, rising as she spoke.

John looked puzzled.

"Funny my having known Broomhurst before, you mean?" he said doubtfully.

"I was fishing down at Lynmouth this time last year," Broomhurst said at dinner. "You know Lynmouth, Mrs. Drayton? Do you never imagine you hear the gurgling of the stream? I am tantalised already by the sound of it rushing through the beautiful green gloom of those woods—*aren't* they lovely? And *I* haven't been in this burnt-up spot as many hours as you've had months of it."

She smiled a little.

"You must learn to possess your soul in patience," she said, and glanced inconsequently from Broomhurst to her husband, and then dropped her eyes and was silent a moment.

John was obviously, and a little audibly, enjoying his dinner. He sat with his chair pushed close to the table, and his elbows awkwardly raised, swallowing his soup in gulps. He grasped his spoon tightly in his bony hand so that its swollen joints stood out larger and uglier than ever, his wife thought.

Her eyes wandered to Broomhurst's hands. They were well shaped, and though not small, there was a look of refinement about them; he had a way of touching things delicately, a little lingeringly, she noticed. There was an air of distinction about his clear-cut, clean-shaven face, possibly intensified by contrast with Drayton's blurred features; and it was, perhaps, also by contrast with the grey cuffs that showed beneath John's ill-cut drab suit that the linen Broomhurst wore seemed to her particularly spotless.

Broomhurst's thoughts, for his part, were a good deal occupied with his hostess.

She was pretty, he thought, or perhaps it was that, with the wide dry lonely plain as a setting, her fragile delicacy of appearance was invested with a certain flower-like charm.

"The silence here seems rather strange, rather appalling at first, when one is fresh from a town," he pursued, after a moment's pause, "but I suppose you're used to it; eh, Drayton? How do *you* find life here, Mrs. Drayton?" he asked a little curiously, turning to her as he spoke.

She hesitated a second. "Oh, much the same as I should find it anywhere else, I expect," she replied; "after all, one carries the possibilities of a happy life about with one—don't you think so? The Garden of

Eden wouldn't necessarily make my life any happier, or less happy, than a howling wilderness like this. It depends on oneself entirely."

"Given the right Adam and Eve, the desert blossoms like the rose, in fact," Broomhurst answered lightly, with a smiling glance inclusive of husband and wife; "you two don't feel as though you'd been driven out of Paradise evidently."

Drayton raised his eyes from his plate with a smile of total incomprehension.

"Great Heavens! What an Adam to select!" thought Broomhurst involuntarily, as Mrs. Drayton rose rather suddenly from the table.

"I'll come and help with that packing-case," John said, rising, in his turn, lumberingly from his place; "then we can have a smoke—eh? Kathie don't mind, if we sit near the entrance."

The two men went out together, Broomhurst holding the lantern, for the moon had not yet risen. Mrs. Drayton followed them to the doorway, and, pushing the looped-up hanging further aside, stepped out into the cool darkness.

Her heart was beating quickly, and there was a great lump in her throat that frightened her as though she were choking.

"And I am his *wife*—I *belong* to him!" she cried, almost aloud.

Thy Heart's Desire

She pressed both her hands tightly against her breast, and set her teeth, fighting to keep down the rising flood that threatened to sweep away her composure. "Oh, what a fool I am! What an hysterical fool of a woman I am!" she whispered below her breath. She began to walk slowly up and down outside the tent, in the space illumined by the lamplight, as though striving to make her outwardly quiet movements react upon the inward tumult. In a little while she had conquered; she quietly entered the tent, drew a low chair to the entrance, and took up a book, just as footsteps became audible. A moment afterwards Broomhurst emerged from the darkness into the circle of light outside, and Mrs. Drayton raised her eyes from the pages she was turning to greet him with a smile.

"Are your things all right?"

"Oh yes, more or less, thank you. I was a little concerned about a case of books, but it isn't much damaged fortunately. Perhaps I've some you would care to look at?"

"The books will be a godsend," she returned with a sudden brightening of the eyes; "I was getting *desperate*—for books."

"What are you reading now?" he asked, glancing at the volume that lay in her lap.

"It's a Browning. I carry it about a good deal. I

think I like to have it with me, but I don't seem to read it much."

"Are you waiting for a suitable optimistic moment?" Broomhurst inquired smiling.

"Yes, now you mention it, I think that must be why I am waiting," she replied slowly.

"And it doesn't come—even in the Garden of Eden? Surely the serpent, pessimism, hasn't been insolent enough to draw you into conversation with him?" he said lightly.

"There has been no one to converse with at all—when John is away, I mean. I think I should have liked a little chat with the serpent immensely by way of a change," she replied in the same tone.

"Ah, yes," Broomhurst said with sudden seriousness, "it must be unbearably dull for you alone here, with Drayton away all day."

Mrs. Drayton's hand shook a little as she fluttered a page of her open book.

"I should think it quite natural you would be irritated beyond endurance to hear that all's right with the world, for instance, when you were sighing for the long day to pass," he continued.

"I don't mind the day so much—it's the evenings." She abruptly checked the swift words and flushed painfully. "I mean—I've grown stupidly nervous, I think—even when John is here. Oh, you have no idea of the awful *silence* of this place at night," she added, rising hurriedly from her low seat, and moving closer to the doorway. "It is so close, isn't it?" she said almost apologetically. There was silence for quite a minute.

Broomhurst's quick eyes noted the silent momentary clenching of the hands that hung at her side as she stood leaning against the support at the entrance.

"But how stupid of me to give you such a bad impression of the camp—the first evening too," Mrs. Drayton exclaimed presently, and her companion mentally commended the admirable composure of her voice.

"Probably you will never notice that it *is* lonely at all," she continued, "John likes it here. He is immensely interested in his work, you know. I hope *you* are too. If you are interested it is all quite right. I think the climate tries me a little. I never used to be stupid—and nervous. Ah, here's John; he's been round to the kitchen-tent, I suppose."

"Been looking after that fellow cleanin' my gun, my dear," John explained, shambling towards the deck-chair.

Later, Broomhurst stood at his own tent-door. He looked up at the star-sown sky, and the heavy silence seemed to press upon him like an actual, physical burden.

He took his cigar from between his lips presently and looked at the glowing end reflectively before throwing it away.

"Considering that she has been alone with him here for six months, she has herself very well in hand—*very* well in hand," he repeated.

III

It was Sunday morning. John Drayton sat just inside the tent, presumably enjoying his pipe before the heat of the day. His eyes furtively followed his wife as she moved about near him, sometimes passing close to his chair in search of something she had mislaid. There was colour in her cheeks; her eyes, though preoccupied, were bright; there was a lightness and buoyancy in her step which she set to a little dancing air she was humming under her breath.

After a moment or two the song ceased, she began to move slowly, sedately; and as if chilled by a raw breath of air, the light faded from her eyes, which she presently turned towards her husband.

"Why do you look at me?" she asked suddenly.

"I don't know, my dear," he began, slowly and laboriously as was his wont. "I was thinkin' how nice you looked—jest now—much better you know—but somehow"—he was taking long whiffs at his pipe, as usual, between each word, while she stood patiently waiting for him to finish—"somehow, you alter so, my dear—you're quite pale again all of a minute."

She stood listening to him, noticing against her will the more than suspicion of cockney accent and the thick drawl with which the words were uttered.

His eyes sought her face piteously. She noticed that too, and stood before him torn by conflicting emotions, pity and disgust struggling in a hand-to-hand fight within her.

"Mr. Broomhurst and I are going down by the well to sit; it's cooler there. Won't you come?" she said at last gently.

He did not reply for a moment, then he turned his head aside, sharply for him.

"No, my dear, thank you; I'm comfortable enough here," he returned huskily.

She stood over him, hesitating a second, then moved abruptly to the table, from which she took a book.

He had risen from his seat by the time she turned to go out, and he intercepted her timorously.

"Kathie, give me a kiss before you go," he whispered hoarsely. "I—I don't often bother you."

She drew her breath in deeply as he put his arms clumsily about her, but she stood still, and he kissed her on the forehead, and touched the little wavy curls that strayed across it gently with his big trembling fingers.

When he released her she moved at once impetuously to the open doorway. On the threshold she hesitated, paused a moment irresolutely, and then turned back.

"Shall I—Does your pipe want filling, John?" she asked softly.

"No, thank you, my dear."

"Would you like me to stay, read to you, or anything?"

He looked up at her wistfully. "N-no, thank you, I'm not much of a reader, you know, my dear—somehow."

She hated herself for knowing that there would be a "my dear," probably a "somehow" in his reply, and despised herself for the sense of irritated impatience she felt by anticipation, even before the words were uttered.

There was a moment's hesitating silence, broken by the sound of quick firm footsteps without. Broomhurst paused at the entrance, and looked into the tent.

"Aren't you coming, Drayton?" he asked, looking first at Drayton's wife and then swiftly putting in his name with a scarcely perceptible pause. "Too lazy? But you, Mrs. Drayton?"

"Yes, I'm coming," she said.

They left the tent together, and walked some few steps in silence.

Broomhurst shot a quick glance at his companion's face.

"Anything wrong?" he asked presently.

Though the words were ordinary enough, the voice in which they were spoken was in some subtle fashion a different voice from that in which he had talked to her nearly two months ago, though it would have required a keen sense of nice shades in sound to have detected the change.

Mrs. Drayton's sense of niceties in sound was particularly keen, but she answered quietly, "Nothing, thank you."

They did not speak again till the trees round the stone-well were reached.

Broomhurst arranged their seats comfortably beside it.

"Are we going to read or talk?" he asked, looking up at her from his lower place.

"Well, we generally talk most when we arrange to read, so shall we agree to talk to-day for a change, by way of getting some reading done?" she rejoined, smiling. "*You* begin."

Broomhurst seemed in no hurry to avail himself of the permission, he was apparently engrossed in watching the flecks of sunshine on Mrs. Drayton's white dress. The whirring of insects, and the creaking of a Persian wheel somewhere in the neighbourhood, filtered through the hot silence.

Mrs. Drayton laughed after a few minutes; there was a touch of embarrassment in the sound.

"The new plan doesn't answer. Suppose you read as usual, and let me interrupt, also as usual, after the first two lines."

He opened the book obediently, but turned the pages at random.

She watched him for a moment, and then bent a little forward towards him.

"It is my turn now," she said suddenly. "Is anything wrong?"

He raised his head, and their eyes met. There was a pause. "I will be more honest than you," he returned. "Yes, there is."

"What?"

"I've had orders to move on."

She drew back, and her lips whitened, though she kept them steady.

"When do you go?"

"On Wednesday."

There was silence again; the man still kept his eyes on her face.

The whirring of the insects and the creaking of the wheel had suddenly grown so strangely loud and insistent, that it was in a half-dazed fashion she at length heard her name—"*Kathleen!*"

"Kathleen!" he whispered again hoarsely.

She looked him full in the face, and once more their eyes met in a long grave gaze.

The man's face flushed, and he half rose from his seat with an impetuous movement, but Kathleen stopped him with a glance.

"Will you go and fetch my work? I left it in the tent," she said, speaking very clearly and distinctly; "and then will you go on reading? I will find the place while you are gone."

She took the book from his hand, and he rose and stood before her.

There was a mute appeal in his silence, and she raised her head slowly.

Her face was white to the lips, but she looked at him unflinchingly; and without a word he turned and left her.

IV

Mrs. Drayton was resting in the tent on Tuesday afternoon. With the help of cushions and some low chairs she had improvised a couch, on which she lay quietly with her eyes closed. There was a tenseness, however, in her attitude which indicated that sleep was far from her.

Her features seemed to have sharpened during the last few days, and there were hollows in her cheeks. She had been very still for a long time, but all at once with a sudden movement she turned her head and buried her face in the cushions with a groan. Slipping from her place she fell on her knees beside the couch, and put both hands before her mouth to force back the cry that she felt struggling to her lips.

For some moments the wild effort she was making for outward calm, which even when she was alone was her first instinct, strained every nerve and blotted out sight and hearing, and it was not till the sound was very near that she was conscious of the ring of horse's hoofs on the plain.

She raised her head sharply with a thrill of fear, still kneeling, and listened.

There was no mistake. The horseman was riding in hot haste, for the thud of the hoofs followed one another swiftly.

As Mrs. Drayton listened her white face grew whiter, and she began to tremble. Putting out shaking hands, she raised herself by the arms of the folding-chair and stood upright.

Thy Heart's Desire

Nearer and nearer came the thunder of the approaching sound, mingled with startled exclamations and the noise of trampling feet from the direction of the kitchen tent.

Slowly, mechanically almost, she dragged herself to the entrance, and stood clinging to the canvas there. By the time she had reached it, Broomhurst had flung himself from the saddle, and had thrown the reins to one of the men.

Mrs. Drayton stared at him with wide bright eyes as he hastened towards her.

"I thought you—you are not—" she began, and then her teeth began to chatter. "I am so cold!" she said, in a little weak voice.

Broomhurst took her hand, and led her over the threshold back into the tent.

"Don't be so frightened," he implored; "I came to tell you first. I thought it wouldn't frighten you so much as—Your—Drayton is—very ill. They are bringing him. I—"

He paused. She gazed at him a moment with parted lips, then she broke into a horrible discordant laugh, and stood clinging to the back of a chair.

Broomhurst started back.

"Do you understand what I mean?" he whispered. "Kathleen, for God's sake—*don't*—he is *dead*."

He looked over his shoulder as he spoke, her

shrill laughter ringing in his ears. The white glare and dazzle of the plain stretched before him, framed by the entrance to the tent; far off, against the horizon, there were moving black specks, which he knew to be the returning servants with their still burden.

They were bringing John Drayton home.

V

One afternoon, some months later, Broomhurst climbed the steep lane leading to the cliffs of a little English village by the sea. He had already been to the inn, and had been shown by the proprietress the house where Mrs. Drayton lodged.

"The lady was out, but the gentleman would likely find her if he went to the cliffs—down by the bay, or thereabouts," her landlady explained, and, obeying her directions, Broomhurst presently emerged from the shady woodland path on to the hillside overhanging the sea.

He glanced eagerly round him, and then with a sudden quickening of the heart, walked on over the springy heather to where she sat. She turned when the rustling his footsteps made through the bracken was near enough to arrest her attention, and looked up at him as he came. Then she rose slowly and stood waiting for him. He came up to her without a word and seized both her hands, devouring her face with his eyes. Something he saw there repelled him. Slowly he let her hands fall, still looking at her silently. "You are not glad to see me, and I have counted the hours," he said at last in a dull toneless voice.

Her lips quivered. "Don't be angry with me—I can't help it—I'm not glad or sorry for anything now," she answered, and her voice matched his for greyness.

They sat down together on a long flat stone half embedded in a wiry clump of whortleberries. Behind them the lonely hillsides rose, brilliant with yellow bracken and the purple of heather. Before them stretched the wide sea. It was a soft grey day. Streaks of pale sunlight trembled at moments far out on the water. The tide was rising in the little bay above which they sat, and Broomhurst watched the lazy foam-edged waves slipping over the uncovered rocks towards the shore, then sliding back as though for very weariness they despaired of reaching it. The muffled pulsing sound of the sea filled the silence. Broomhurst thought suddenly of hot Eastern sunshine, of the whirr of insect wings on the still air, and the creaking of a wheel in the distance. He turned and looked at his companion.

"I have come thousands of miles to see you," he

said; "aren't you going to speak to me now I am here?"

"Why did you come? I told you not to come," she answered, falteringly. "I—" she paused.

"And I replied that I should follow you—if you remember," he answered, still quietly. "I came because I would not listen to what you said then, at that awful time. You didn't know *yourself* what you said. No wonder! I have given you some months, and now I have come."

There was silence between them. Broomhurst saw that she was crying; her tears fell fast on to her hands, that were clasped in her lap. Her face, he noticed, was thin and drawn.

Very gently he put his arm round her shoulder and drew her nearer to him. She made no resistance—it seemed that she did not notice the movement; and his arm dropped at his side.

"You asked me why I had come? You think it possible that three months can change one, very thoroughly, then?" he said in a cold voice.

"I not only think it possible, I have proved it," she replied wearily.

He turned round and faced her.

"You *did* love me, Kathleen!" he asserted; "you never said so in words, but I know it," he added fiercely.

"Yes, I did."

"And—You mean that you don't now?"

Her voice was very tired. "Yes—I can't help it," she answered, "it has gone—utterly."

The grey sea slowly lapped the rocks. Overhead the sharp scream of a gull cut through the stillness. It was broken again, a moment afterwards, by a short hard laugh from the man.

"Don't!" she whispered, and laid a hand swiftly on his arm. "Do you think it isn't worse for me? I wish to God I *did* love you," she cried passionately. "Perhaps it would make me forget that to all intents and purposes I am a murderess."

Broomhurst met her wide despairing eyes with an amazement which yielded to sudden pitying comprehension.

"So that is it, my darling? You are worrying about *that?* You who were as loyal, as——"

She stopped him with a frantic gesture.

"Don't! *don't!*" she wailed. "If you only knew; let me try to tell you—will you?" she urged pitifully. "It may be better if I tell some one—if I don't keep it all to myself, and think, and *think*."

She clasped her hands tight, with the old gesture he remembered when she was struggling for self-control, and waited a moment.

Presently she began to speak in a low hurried

tone: "It began before you came. I know now what the feeling was that I was afraid to acknowledge to myself. I used to try and smother it, I used to repeat things to myself all day—poems, stupid rhymes—*anything* to keep my thoughts quite underneath—but I—*hated* John before you came! We had been married nearly a year then. I never loved him. Of course you are going to say: 'Why did you marry him?'" She looked drearily over the placid sea. "Why *did* I marry him? I don't know; for the reason that hundreds of ignorant inexperienced girls marry, I suppose. My home wasn't a happy one. I was miserable, and oh,—*restless*. I wonder if men know what it feels like to be restless? Sometimes I think they can't even guess. John wanted me very badly—nobody wanted me at home particularly. There didn't seem to be any point in my life. Do you understand? . . . . Of course being alone with him in that little camp in that silent plain"—she shuddered—"made things worse. My nerves went all to pieces. Everything he said—his voice—his accent—his walk—the way he ate—irritated me so that I longed to rush out sometimes and shriek—and go *mad*. Does it sound ridiculous to you to be driven mad by such trifles? I only know I used to get up from the table sometimes and walk up and down outside, with both hands over my mouth to keep myself quiet. And all the time I *hated* myself—how I hated myself! I never had a word from him that wasn't gentle and tender. I believe he loved the ground I walked on. Oh, it is *awful* to be loved like that, when you—" She drew in her breath with a sob. "I—I—it made me sick for him to come near me—to touch me." She stopped a moment.

Broomhurst gently laid his hand on her quivering one. "Poor little girl!" he murmured.

"Then *you* came," she said, "and before long I had another feeling to fight against. At first I thought it couldn't be true that I loved you—it would die down. I think I was *frightened* at the feeling; I didn't know it hurt so to love any one."

Broomhurst stirred a little. "Go on," he said tersely.

"But it didn't die," she continued in a trembling whisper, "and the other *awful* feeling grew stronger and stronger—hatred; no, that is not the word—*loathing* for—for—John. I fought against it. Yes," she cried feverishly, clasping and unclasping her hands, "Heaven knows I fought it with all my strength, and reasoned with myself, and—oh, I did *everything*, but—" Her quick-falling tears made speech difficult.

"Kathleen!" Broomhurst urged desperately, "you couldn't help it, you poor child. You say yourself you struggled against your feelings—you were always gentle. Perhaps he didn't know."

"But he did—he *did*," she wailed, "it is just that. I hurt him a hundred times a day; he never said so, but I knew it; and yet I *couldn't* be kind to him—except in words—and he understood. And after you came it was worse in one way, for he knew. I *felt* he knew that I loved you. His eyes used to follow me like a dog's, and I was stabbed with remorse, and I tried to be good to him, but I couldn't."

"But—he didn't suspect—he trusted you," began Broomhurst. "He had every reason. No woman was ever so loyal, so—"

"Hush," she almost screamed. "Loyal! it was the least I could do—to stop you, I mean—when you— After all, I knew it without your telling me. I had deliberately married him without loving him. It was my own fault. I felt it. Even if I couldn't prevent his knowing that I hated him, I could prevent *that*. It was my punishment. I deserved it for *daring* to marry without love. But I didn't spare John one pang after all," she added bitterly. "He knew what I felt towards him—I don't think he cared about anything else. You say I mustn't reproach myself? When I went back to the tent that morning—when you—when I stopped you from saying you loved me, he was sitting at the table with his head buried in his hands; he was crying—bitterly: I saw him—it is terrible to see a man cry—and I stole away gently, but he saw me. I was torn to pieces, but I *couldn't* go to him. I knew he would kiss me, and I shuddered to think of it. It seemed more than ever not to be borne that he should do that—when I knew *you* loved me."

"Kathleen," cried her lover again, "don't dwell on it all so terribly—don't—"

"How can I forget?" she answered despairingly, "and then"—she lowered her voice—"oh, I can't tell you—all the time, at the back of my mind somewhere, there was a burning wish that he might *die*. I used to lie awake at night, and do what I would to stifle it, that thought used to *scorch* me, I wished it so intensely. Do you believe that by willing one can bring such things to pass?" she asked, looking at Broomhurst with feverishly bright eyes. "No?—well, I don't know—I tried to smother it. I *really* tried, but it was there, whatever other thoughts I heaped on the top. Then, when I heard the horse galloping across the plain that morning, I had a sick fear that it was *you*. I knew something had happened, and my first thought when I saw you alive and well, and knew that it was *John*, was, *that it was too good to be true*. I believe I laughed like a maniac, didn't I? . . . . Not to blame? Why, if it hadn't been for me he wouldn't have died. The men say they saw him sitting with his head uncovered in the burning sun, his face buried in his hands—just as I had seen him the day before. He didn't trouble to be careful—he was too wretched."

She paused, and Broomhurst rose and began to pace the little hillside path at the edge of which they were seated.

Presently he came back to her.

"Kathleen, let me take care of you," he implored, stooping towards her. "We have only ourselves to consider in this matter. Will you come to me at once?"

She shook her head sadly.

Broomhurst set his teeth, and the lines round his mouth deepened. He threw himself down beside her on the heather.

"Dear," he urged still gently, though his voice showed he was controlling himself with an effort. "You are morbid about this. You have been alone too much—you are ill. Let me take care of you: I *can*, Kathleen—and I love you. Nothing but morbid fancy makes you imagine you are in any way responsible for—Drayton's death. You can't bring him back to life, and—"

"No," she sighed drearily, "and if I could, nothing would be altered. Though I am mad with self-reproach, I feel *that*—it was all so inevitable. If he were alive and well before me this instant my feeling towards him wouldn't have changed. If he spoke to me, he would say 'My dear'—and I should *loathe* him. Oh, I know! It is *that* that makes it so awful."

"But if you acknowledge it," Broomhurst struck in eagerly, "will you wreck both of our lives for the sake of vain regrets? Kathleen, you never will."

He waited breathlessly for her answer.

"I won't wreck both our lives by marrying again without love on my side," she replied firmly.

"I will take the risk," he said. "You *have* loved me—you will love me again. You are crushed and dazed now with brooding over this—this trouble, but—"

"But I will not allow you to take the risk," Kathleen answered. "What sort of woman should I be to be willing again to live with a man I don't love? I have come to know that there are things one owes to *oneself*. Self-respect is one of them. I don't know how it has come to be so, but all my old feeling for you has *gone*. It is as though it had burnt itself out. I will not offer grey ashes to any man."

Broomhurst looking up at her pale, set face, knew that her words were final, and turned his own aside with a groan.

"Ah!" cried Kathleen with a little break in her voice, "*don't*. Go away and be happy and strong, and all that I loved in you. I am so sorry—so sorry to hurt you. I—" her voice faltered miserably. "I—I only bring trouble to people."

There was a long pause.

"Did you never think that there is a terrible vein of irony running through the ordering of this world?" she said presently. "It is a mistake to think our prayers are not answered—they are. In due time we get our heart's desire—when we have ceased to care for it."

"I haven't yet got mine," Broomhurst answered doggedly, "and I shall never cease to care for it."

She smiled a little with infinite sadness.

"Listen, Kathleen," he said. They had both risen and he stood before her, looking down at her. "I will go now, but in a year's time I shall come back. I will not give you up. You shall love me yet."

"Perhaps—I don't think so," she answered wearily.

Broomhurst looked at her trembling lips a moment in silence, then he stooped and kissed both her hands instead.

"I will wait till you tell me you love me," he said.

She stood watching him out of sight. He did not look back, and she turned with swimming eyes to the grey sea and the transient gleams of sunlight that swept like tender smiles across its face.

Lionel Johnson

Tobacco Clouds

Cloud upon cloud: and, if I were to think that an image of life can lie in wreathing, blue tobacco smoke, pleasant were the life so fancied. Its fair changes in air, its gentle motions, its quiet dying out and away at last, should symbolise something more than perfect idleness. Cloud upon cloud: and I will think, as I have said: it is amusing to think so.

It is that death, out and away upon the air, which charms me: charms more than the manner of the blown red rose, full of dew at morning, upon the grass at sunset. The clouds' end, their death in air, fills me with a very beauty of desire; it has no violence in it, and it is almost invisible. Think of it! While the cloud lived, it was seemly and various; and with a graceful change it passed away: the image of a reasonable life is there, hanging among tobacco clouds. An image and a test: an image, because elaborated by fancy: a true and appealing image, and so, to my present way of life, a test.

That way is, to walk about the old city, with "a

spirit in my feet," as Shelley and Catullus have it, of joyous aims and energies; and to speed home to my solitary room over the steep High Street; in an armchair, to read Milton and Lucretius, with others. There is nothing unworthy in all this: there is open air, an ancient city, a lonely chamber, perfect poets. Those should make up a passing life well: for death! I can watch tobacco clouds, exploring the secret of their beautiful conclusion. And, indeed, I think that already this life has something of their manner, those wheeling clouds! It has their light touch upon the world, and certainly their harmlessness. Early morning, when the dew sparkles red; honey, and coffee, and eggs for a breakfast; the quick, eager walk between the limes, through the Close of fine grass, to the river fields; then the blithe return to my poets; all that, together, comes to resemble the pleasant spheres of tobacco cloud; I mean, the circling hours, in their passage, and in their change, have something of a dreamy order and progression. Such little incidents! Now, grey air and whistling leaves: now, a marketing crowd of country folk round the Cross: and presently, clear candles; with Milton, in rich Baskervile type, or Lucretius, in the exquisite print of early Italy.

Such little incidents, in a world of battles and of plagues: of violent death by sea and land! Yet this quiet life, too, has difficulties and needs: its changes must be gone through with a ready pleasure and a mind unhesitating. For, trivial though they be in aspect and amount, yet the consecration of them, to be an holy discipline of experience, is so much the greater an attempt: it is an art. Each thing, be it man, or book, or place, should have its rights, when it encounters me: each has its proper quality, its peculiar spirit, not to be misinterpreted by me in carelessness, nor overlooked with impatience. That is clear: but neither must I vaunt my just view of common life. Meditation, at twilight, by the window looking toward the bare downs, is very different from that anxious examination of motives, dear to sedulous souls. My meditation is only still life: the clouds of smoke go up, grey and blue; the earlier stars come out, above the sunset and the melancholy downs; and deep, mournful bells ring slowly among the valley trees. Then, if my day have been successful, what peace follows, and how profound a charm! The little things of the day, sudden glances of light upon grey stone, pleasant snatches of organ music from the church, quaint rustic sights in some near village: they come back upon me, gentle touches of happiness, airs of repose. And when the mysteries come about me, the fearfulness of life, and the shadow of night; then, have I not still the blue, grey clouds, *occultis de rebus quo referam?* So I escape the tribulations of doubt, those gloomy tribulations: and I live in the strength of dreams, which never doubt.

Is it all a delusion? But that is a foolish wonder: nothing is a delusion, except the extremes of pleasure and of pain. Take what you will of the world; its crowds, or its calms: there is nothing altogether wrong to every one. Lucretius, upon his watchtower, deny it as he may, found some exultation and delight in the lamentable prospect below: it filled him with a magnificent darkness of soul, a princely compassion at heart. And Milton, in his evil days, felt himself to be tragic and austere: he knew it, not as a proud boast, but as a proud fact. No! life is never wrong, altogether, to every one: you and I, he and she, priest and penitent, master and slave: one with another, we compose a very glory of existence before the unseen Powers. Therefore, I believe in my measured way of life; its careful felicities, fashioned out of little things: to you, the change of Ministries, and the accomplishment of conquests, bring their wealth of rich emotion: to me, who am apart from the louder concerns of life, the flowering of the limes, and the warm autumn rains, bring their pensive beauty and a store of memories.

Is it I, am indolent? Is it you, are clamorous? Why

should it be either? Let us say, I am the lover of quiet things, and you are enamoured of mighty events. Each, without undue absorption in his taste, relishes the savour of a different experience.

But I think, I am no egoist: no melancholy spectator of things, cultivating his intellect with old poetry, nourishing his senses upon rural nature. There are times, when the swarms of men press hard upon a solitary; he hears the noise of the streets, the heavy vans of merchandise, the cry of the railway whistle: and in a moment, his thoughts travel away, to London, to Liverpool; to great docks and to great ships; and away, till he is watching the dissimilar bustle of Eastern harbours, and hearing the discordant sounds of Chinese workmen. The blue smoke curls and glides away, with blue pagodas, and snowy almond bloom, and cherry flowers, circling and gleaming in it, like a narcotic vision. O magic of tobacco! Dreams are there, and superb images, and a somnolent paradise. Sometimes, the swarms of humanity press wearily and hardly; with a cruel insistence, crushing out my right to happiness. I think, rather I brood, upon the fingers that deftly rolled the cigarette, upon the people in tobacco plantations, upon all the various commerce involved in its history: how do they all fare, those many workers? Strolling up and down, devouring my books through their lettered backs; remembering the workers with leather, paper, ink, who toiled at them, they frighten me from the peace. What a full world it is! What endless activities there are! And, oh, Nicomachean Ethics! how much conscious pleasure is in them all! Things, mere tangible things, have a terrible power of education: of calling out from the mind innumerable thoughts and sympathies. Like childish catechisms and categories—*Whence have we sago?*—plain substances introduce me to swarms of men, before unrealised. And they all lived and died, and cared for their children, or not, and led reasonable lives, or not: and, without any alternative, had casual thoughts and constant passions. Did each one of them ever stop in his work, and think that the world revolved about him alone; and all was his, and for him? Most men may have thought so, and shivered a little afterwards; and worked on steadily. Or did each one of them ever think that he was always beset with companions, hordes of men and women, necessary and inevitable? Then, he must have struggled a little in his mind, as a man fights for air, and worked on steadily. It does not do: this interrogation of mysteries, which are also facts. Nor am I called upon, from without or from within, to write an Essay upon the Problem of Economic Distribution. *Præsentia temnis!* Nature says to me: it is the stir of the world, and the great play of forces, that I am wailing, to no end. Let the great life continue, and the sun shine upon bright palaces; and geraniums, red geraniums, glow at the windows of dingy courts; death and sorrow come upon both, and upon me. And on all sides there is infinite tenderness; the invincible good-will, which says kind and cheerful things to every one sometimes, by a friend's mouth; the humane pieties of the world, which make glad the *Civitas Dei*, and make endurable the *Regnum Hominis*. I need not make myself miserable.

Full night at last; the dead of night, as dull folk have it; ignorant persons, who know nothing of nocturnal beauty, of night's lively magic. It was a good thought, to come out of my lonely room, to look at the cloisters by moonlight, and to wander round the Close, under the black shadows of the buttresses, while the moon is white upon their strange pinnacles. There is no noise, but only a silence, which seems very old; old, as the grey monuments and the weathered arches. The wreathing, blue tobacco clouds look thin and pale, like breath upon a dark frosty night; they drift about these old precincts, with a kind of uncertainty and discomfort; one would think, they wanted a rich Mediterranean night, heavy odours of roses, and very fiery stars.

Instead, they break upon mouldering traceries, and doleful cherubs of the last century; upon sunken headstones, and black oak doors with ironwork over them. Perhaps the cigarette is southern and Latin, southern and Oriental, after all; and I am a dreamer, out of place in this northern grey antiquity. If it be so, I can taste the subtle pleasures of contrast: and, dwelling upon the singular features of this old town, I can make myself a place in it, as its conscious critic and adopted alien. There is a curious apprehension of enjoyment, a genuine touch of luxury, in this nocturnal visit to these old northern things! I consider, with satisfaction, how the Stuart king, who spurned tobacco contumeliously, put a devoted faith in witches, those northern daughters of the devil; northern, and very different from the dames of Thessaly; from the crones of Propertius, and of Horace, and of Apuleius the Golden. Who knows, but I may hear strange voices in the near aisle before cockcrow? By night, night in the north, happen cold and dismal things; and then, what a night is this! Chilly stars, and wild, grey clouds, flying over a misty moon.

At last, here comes a great and solemn sound; the commanding bells of the cathedral tower, in their iron, midnight toll. Through the sombre strokes, and striking into their long echoes, pierce the thin cries of bats, that wheel in air, like lost creatures who hate themselves; the uncanny flitter-mice! They trace superb, invisible circles on the night; crying out faintly and plaintively, with no sort of delight in their voices: things of keen teeth, furry bodies, and skeleton wings covered scantily in leather. The big moths, too: they blunder against my face, and dash red trails of fire off my cigarette; so busily they spin about the darkness. *Sadducismus triumphatus!* Yes, truly: here are little, white spirits awake and at some faery work; white, as heather upon the Cornish cliffs is white, and all innocent, rare things in heaven and earth. There is nothing dreadful, it seems, about this night, and this place; no glorious fury of evil spirits, doing foul and ugly things; only the quiet town asleep under a wild sky, and gentle creatures of the night moving about ancient places. And the wind rises, with a sound of the sea, murmuring over the earth and sighing away to the sea: the trembling sea, beyond the downs, which steals into the land by great creeks and glimmering channels; with swaying, taper masts along them, and lantern lights upon black barges. Certainly, this is no Lucretian night: not that tremendous

> *Nox, et noctis signa severa*
> *Noctivagæque faces cœli, flammæque volantes.*

Rather, it reminds me of the Miltonic night, which is peopled alluringly with

> "faery elves,
> Whose midnight revels by a forest side
> Or fountain, some belated peasant sees,
> Or dreams he sees, while overhead the moon
> Sits arbitress:"

a Miltonic night, and a Shakespearean dawn; for the white morning has just peered along the horizon, white morning, with dusky flames behind it; and the spirits, the visions, vanish away, "following darkness, like a dream."

The streets are very still, with that silence of sleeping cities, which seems ready to start into confused cries; as though the Smiter of the Firstborn were travelling through the households. There is the Catholic chapel, in its Georgian, quaint humility; recalling an age of beautiful, despised simplicity; the age of French emigrant old priests and vicars-apostolic, who stood for the Supreme Pontiff, in grey wigs. The sweet limes are swaying against its singular, umbered windows, with their holy saints and prophets in last-century design; ruffled, querulous persons looking very bluff and blown. I wonder, how it would be inside; I suppose, night has a little weakened that lingering smell of daily incense, which seems so immemorial and so sad. Wonderful grace of the mighty Roman Church! This low square place, where the sanctuary is poor and open, without any mystical touch of retirement and of loftiness, has yet the unfailing charm, the venerable mystery, which attend the footsteps of the Church; the same air of command, the same look of pleading, fill this homely, comfortable shrine, which simple country gentlemen set up for the ministrations of harassed priests, in an age of no enthusiasm. I like to think that this quiet chapel, in the obedience of Rome, in communion with that supreme apostolate, is always open to me upon this winding little by-street; it fills me with perfect memories, and it seems to bless me.

But here is a benediction of light! the quick sun, reddening half the heavens, and rising gloriously. In the valley, clusters of elm rock and swing with the breeze, quivering for joy: far away, the bare uplands roll against the sunrise, calm and pastoral; *otia dia* of the morning. Surely the hours have gone well, and according to my preference; one dying into another, as the tobacco clouds die. My meditations, too, have been peaceful enough; and, though solitary, I have had fine companions. What would the moral philosophers, those puzzled sages, think of me? An harmless hedonist? An amateur in morals, who means well, though meaning very little? Nay! let the moralist by profession give, to whom he will, *sa musique, sa flamme*: to any practical person, who is a wise shareholder and zealous vestryman. For myself, my limited and dreamy self, I eschew these upright businesses; upright memories and meditations please me more, and to live with as little action as may be. Action: why do they talk of action? Match me, for pure activity, one evening of my dreams, when life and death fill my mind with their messengers, and the days of old come back to me. And now, homewards, for a little sleep; that profound and rich slumber at early dawn which is my choice delight. A sleep, bathed in musical impressions, and filled with fresh dreams, all impossible and happy; four hours, and five, and six perhaps: then the cathedral matin bell will chime in with my fancies, and I shall wake harmoniously. I shall feel infinitely cheerful, after the spirit of the *Compleat Angler*; I shall remember that I was once at Ware, and at Amwell, those placid haunts of Walton. A conviction of beauty, and contentment in life will lay hold on me, more than commonly; it is probable that I shall read *The Spectator*, and Addison, rather than Steele, at breakfast. And I know which paper it will be: it will be about *Will Wimble* coming up to the house, with two or three hazel twigs in his hand, fresh cut in *Sir Roger's* woods. Or, if I prove faithful to my great

Lucretius: the man, not the book, for I read him in the Giuntine: I will read that marvellous *It ver et Venus*; that dancing masque of beauty. For *L'Allegro*, I do not read that; it is read aloud to me by the morning, with exquisite, bright cadences. After my honey from the flowers of a very rustic farm, and my coffee, from some wonderful Eastern place; and my eggs, marked by the careful housewife as she took them from her henhouse, covered with stonecrop over its old tiles; after all these delicates, now comes the first cigarette, pungent and exhilarating. As the grey blue clouds go up, the ruddy sunlight glows through them, straight as an arrow through the gold. Away they wander, out of the window, flung back upon the air, against the roses, and disappear in the buoyant morning.

My thoughts go with them, into the morning, into all the mornings over the world. They travel through the lands, and across the seas, and are everywhere at home, enjoying the presence of life. And past things, old histories, are turned to pleasant recollections: a *pot-pourri*, justly seasoned, and subtly scented; the evil humours and the monstrous tyrannies pass away, and leave only the happiness and the peace.

Call me, my dear friend, what reproachful name you please; but, by your leave, the world is better for my cheerfulness. True, should the terrible issues come upon me, demanding high courage, and finding but good temper, then give me your prayers, for I have my misdoubts. Till then, let me cultivate my place in life, nurturing its comelier flowers; taking the little things of time with a grateful relish and a mind at rest. So hours and years pass into hours and years, gently, and surely, and orderly; as these clouds, grey and blue clouds, of tobacco smoke, pass up to the air, and away upon the wind; incense of a goodly savour, cheering the thoughts of my heart, before passing away, to disappear at last.

Ella D'Arcy

The Death Mask

The Master was dead; and Peschi, who had come round to the studio to see about some repairs—part of the ceiling had fallen owing to the too lively proceedings of Dubourg and his eternal visitors overhead—Peschi displayed a natural pride that it was he who had been selected from among the many *mouleurs* of the Quarter, to take a mask of the dead man.

All Paris was talking of the Master, although not, assuredly, under that title. All Paris was talking of his life, of his genius, of his misery, and of his death. Peschi, for the moment, was sole possessor of valuable unedited details, to the narration of which Hiram P. Corner, who had dropped in to pass the evening with me, listened with keenly attentive ears.

Corner was a recent addition to the American Art Colony; ingenuous as befitted his eighteen years, and of a more than improbable innocence. Paris, to him, represented the Holiest of Holies; the dead

Master, by the adorable impeccability of his writings, figuring therein as one of the High Priests. Needless to say, he had never come in contact with that High Priest, had never even seen him; while the Simian caricatures which so frequently embellished the newspapers, made as little impression on the lad's mind as did the unequivocal allusions, jests, and epigrams, for ever flung up like sea-spray against the rock of his unrevered name.

The absorbing interest Corner felt glowed visibly on his fresh young western face, and it was this, I imagine, which led Peschi to propose that we should go back with him to his *atelier* and see the mask for ourselves.

Peschi is a Genoese; small, lithe, very handsome; a skilled workman, a little demon of industry; full of enthusiasms, with the real artist-soul. He works for Felon the sculptor, and it was Felon who had been commissioned to do the bust for which the death mask would serve as model.

It is always pleasant to hear Peschi talk; and to-night, as we walked from the Rue Fleurus to the Rue Notre-Dame-des-Champs he told us something of mask-taking in general, with illustrations from this particular case.

On the preceding day, barely two hours after death had taken place, Rivereau, one of the dead man's intimates, had rushed into Peschi's workroom, and carried him off, with the necessary materials, to the Rue Monsieur, in a cab. Rivereau, though barely twenty, is perhaps the most notorious of the *bande*. Peschi described him to Corner as having dark, evil, narrow eyes set too close together in a perfectly white face, framed by falling, lustreless black hair; and with the stooping shoulders, the troubled walk, the attenuated hands common to his class.

Arrived at the house, Rivereau led the way up the dark and dirty staircase to the topmost landing, and as they paused there an instant, Peschi could hear the long-drawn, hopeless sobs of a woman within the door.

On being admitted he found himself in an apartment consisting of two small, inconceivably squalid rooms, opening one from the other.

In the outer room, five or six figures, the disciples, friends, and lovers of the dead poet, conversed together; a curious group in a medley of costumes. One in an opera-hat, shirt-sleeves, and soiled grey trousers tied up with a bit of stout string; another in a black coat buttoned high to conceal the fact that he wore no shirt at all; a third in clothes crisp from the tailor, with an immense bunch of Parma violets in his buttonhole. But all were alike in the strangeness of their eyes, their voices, their gestures.

Seen through the open door of the further room, lay the corpse under a sheet, and by the bedside knelt the stout, middle-aged mistress, whose sobs had reached the stairs.

Madame Germaine, as she was called in the Quarter, had loved the Master with that complete, self-abnegating, sublime love of which certain women are capable—a love uniting that of the mother, the wife, and the nurse all in one. For years she had cooked for him, washed for him, mended for him; had watched through whole nights by his bedside when he was ill; had suffered passively his blows, his reproaches, and his neglect, when, thanks to her care, he was well again. She adored him dumbly, closed her eyes to his vices, and magnified his gifts, without in the least comprehending them. She belonged to the *ouvrière* class, could not read, could not write her own name; but with a characteristic which is as French as it is un-British, she paid her homage to intellect, where an Englishwoman only gives it to inches and muscle. Madame Germaine was prouder perhaps of the Master's greatness, worshipped him more devoutly, than any one of the super-cultivated, ultra-corrupt group, who by their flatteries and complaisances had assisted him to his ruin.

It was with the utmost difficulty, Peschi said, that

Rivereau and the rest had succeeded in persuading the poor creature to leave the bedside and go into the other room while the mask was being taken.

The operation, it seems, is a sufficiently horrible one, and no relative is permitted to be present. As you cover the dead face over with the plaster, a little air is necessarily forced back again into the lungs, and this air as it passes along the windpipe causes strange rattlings, sinister noises, so that you might swear that the corpse was returned to life. Then, as the mould is removed, the muscles of the face drag and twitch, the mouth opens, the tongue lolls out; and Peschi declared that this always remains for him a gruesome moment. He has never accustomed himself to it; on every recurring occasion it fills him with the same repugnance; and this, although he has taken so many masks, is so deservedly celebrated for them, that *la bande* had instantly selected him to perpetuate the Master's lineaments.

"But it's an excellent likeness," said Peschi; "you see they sent for me so promptly that he had not changed at all. He does not look as though he were dead, but just asleep."

Meanwhile we had reached the unshuttered shop-front, where Peschi displays, on Sundays and week-days alike, his finished works of plastic art to the *gamins* and *filles* of the Quarter.

Looking past the statuary, we could see into the living-room beyond, it being separated from the shop only by a glass partition. It was lighted by a lamp set in the centre of the table, and in the circle of light thrown from beneath its green shade, we saw a charming picture: the young head of Madame Peschi bent over her baby, whom she was feeding at the breast. She is eighteen, pretty as a rose, and her story and Peschi's is an idyllic one; to be told, perhaps, another time. She greeted us with the smiling, cordial, unaffected kindliness which in France warms your blood with the constant sense of brotherhood; and, giving the boy to his father—a delicious opalescent trace of milk hanging about the little mouth—she got up to see about another lamp which Peschi had asked for.

Holding this lamp to guide our steps, he preceded us now across a dark yard to his workshop at the further end, and while we went we heard the young mother's exquisite nonsense-talk addressed to the child, as she settled back in her place again to her nursing.

Peschi, unlocking a door, flashed the light down a long room, the walls of which, the trestle-tables, the very floor, were hung, laden, and encumbered with a thousand heterogeneous objects. Casts of every description and dimension, finished, unfinished, broken; scrolls for ceilings; caryatides for chimney-pieces; cornucopias for the entablatures of buildings; chubby Cupids jostling emaciated Christs; broken columns for Père Lachaise, or consolatory upward-pointing angels; hands, feet, and noses for the Schools of Art; a pensively posed *écorché* contemplating a Venus of Milo fallen upon her back; these, and a crowd of nameless, formless things, seemed to spring at our eyes, as Peschi raised or lowered the lamp, moved it this way or the other.

"There it is," said he, pointing forwards; and I saw lying flat upon a modelling-board, with upturned features, a grey, immobile simulacrum of the curiously mobile face I remembered so well.

"Of course you must understand," said Paschi, "it's only in the rough, just exactly as it came from the *creux*. Fifty copies are to be cast altogether, and this is the first one. But I must prop it up for you. You can't judge of it as it is."

He looked about him for a free place on which to set the lamp. Not finding any, he put it down on the floor. For a few moments he stood busied over the mask with his back to us.

"Now you can see it properly," said he, and stepped aside.

The lamp threw its rays upwards, illuminating strongly the lower portion of the cast, throwing the upper portion into deepest shadow, with the effect that the inanimate mask was become suddenly a living face, but a face so unutterably repulsive, so hideously bestial, that I grew cold to the roots of my hair. . . . A fat, loose throat, a retreating chinless chin, smeared and bleared with the impressions of the meagre beard; a vile mouth, lustful, flaccid, the lower lip disproportionately great; ignoble lines; hateful puffinesses; something inhuman and yet worse than inhuman in its travesty of humanity; something that made you hate the world and your fellows, that made you hate yourself for being ever so little in *this* image. A more abhorrent spectacle I have never seen. . . .

So soon as I could turn my eyes from the ghastly thing, I looked at Corner. He was white as the plaster faces about him. His immensely opened eyes showed his astonishment and his terror. For what I experienced was intensified in his case by the unexpected and complete disillusionment. He had opened the door of the tabernacle, and out had crawled a noisome spider; he had lifted to his lips the communion cup, and therein squatted a toad. A sort of murmur of frantic protestation began to rise in his throat; but Peschi, unconscious of our agitation, now lifted the lamp, passed round with it behind the mask, held it high, and let the rays stream downwards from above.

The astounding way the face changed must have been seen to be believed in. It was exactly as though, by some cunning sleight of hand, the mask of a god had been substituted for that of a satyr. . . . You saw a splendid dome-like head, Shakespearean in contour; a broad, smooth, finely-modelled brow; thick, regular, horizontal eyebrows, casting a shadow which diminished the too great distance separating them from the eyes; while the deeper shadow thrown below the nose altered its character entirely. Its snout-like appearance was gone, its deep, wide-open, upturned nostrils were hidden, but you noticed the well-marked transition from forehead to nose-base, the broad ridge denoting extraordinary mental power. Over the eyeballs the lids had slidden down smooth and creaseless; the little tell-tale palpebral wrinkles which had given such libidinous lassitude to the eye had vanished away. The lips no longer looked gross, and they closed together in a beautiful, sinuous line, now first revealed by the shadow on the upper one. The prominence of the jaws, the muscularity of the lower part of the face, which gave it so painfully microcephalous an appearance, were now unnoticeable; on the contrary, the whole face looked small beneath the noble head and brow. You remarked the medium-sized and well-formed ears, with the "swan" distinct in each, the gently-swelling breadth of head above them, the full development of the forehead over the orbits of the eyes. You discerned the presence of those higher qualities which might have rendered him an ascetic or a saint; which led him to understand the beauty of self-denial, to appreciate the wisdom of self-restraint: and you did not see how these qualities remained inoperative in him, being completely over-balanced by the size of the lower brain, the thick, bull throat, and the immense length from the ear to the base of the skull at the back.

I had often seen the Master in life: I had seen him sipping *absinthe* at the d'Harcourt; reeling, a Silemus-like figure, among the nocturnal Bacchantes of the Boul' Miche; lying in the gutter outside his house, until his mistress should come to pick him up and take him in. I had seen in the living man more traces than a few of the bestiality which the death-mask had completely verified; but never in the living man had I suspected anything of the beauty, of the splendour, that I now saw.

For that the Master had somewhere a beautiful soul you divined from his works; from the exquisite melody of all of them, from the pure, the ecstatic, the religious altitude of some few. But in actual daily life, his loose and violent will-power, his insane passions, held that soul bound down so close a captive, that those who knew him best were the last to admit its existence.

And here, a mere accident of lighting displayed not only that existence, but its visible, outward expression as well. In these magnificent lines and arches of head and brow, you saw what the man might have been, what God had intended him to be; what his mother had foreseen in him, when, a tiny infant like Peschi's yonder, she had cradled the warm, downy, sweet-smelling little head upon her bosom, and dreamed day-dreams of all the high, the great, the wonderful things her boy later on was to do. You saw what the poor, purblind, middle-aged mistress was the only one to see in the seamed and ravaged face she kissed so tenderly for the last time before the coffin-lid was closed.

You saw the head of gold; you could forget the feet of clay, or, remembering them, you found for the first time some explanation of the anomalies of his career.

You understood how he who could pour out passionate protestations of love and devotion to God in the morning, offering up body and soul, flesh and blood in his service; dedicating his brow as a footstool for the Sacred Feet; his hands as censers for the glowing coals, the precious incense; condemning his eyes, misleading lights, to be extinguished by the tears of prayer; you understood how, nevertheless, before evening was come, he would set every law of God and decency at defiance, use every member, every faculty, in the service of sin.

It was given to him, as it is given to few, to see the Best, to reverence it, to love it; and the blind, groping hesitatingly forward in the darkness, do not stray as far as he strayed.

He knew the value of work, its imperative necessity; that in the sweat of his brow the artist, like the day-labourer, must produce, must produce: and he spent his slothful days shambling from café to café.

He never denied his vices; he recognised them and found excuses for them, high moral reasons even, as the intellectual man can always do. To indulge them was but to follow out the dictates of Nature, who in herself is holy; cynically to expose them to the world was but to be absolutely sincere.

And his disciples, going further, taught with a vague poetic mysticism that he was a fresh Incarnation of the Godhead; that what was called his immorality was merely his scorn of truckling to the base conventions of the world. But in his saner moments he described himself more accurately as a man blown hither and thither by the winds of evil chance, just as a withered leaf is blown in autumn; and having received great and exceptional gifts, with Shakespeare's length of years in which to turn them to account, he had chosen instead to wallow in such vileness that his very name was anathema among honourable men.

Chosen? Did he choose? Can one say after all that he chose to resemble the leaf rather than the tree? The gates of gifts close on the child with the womb, and all we possess comes to us from afar, and is collected from a thousand diverging sources.

If that splendid head and brow were contained in the seed, so also were the retreating chin, the debased jaw, the animal mouth. One as much as the other was the direct inheritance of former generations. Considered in a certain aspect, it seems that a man by taking thought, may as little hope to thwart the implanted propensities of his character, as to alter the shape of his skull or the size of his jawbone.

I lost myself in mazes of predestination and free-will. Life appeared to me as a huge kaleidoscope turned by the hand of Fate. The atoms of glass coalesce into patterns, fall apart, unite together again, are always the same, but always different, and, shake the glass never so slightly, the precise combination you have just been looking at is broken up for ever. It can never be repeated. This particular man, with his faults and his virtues, his unconscious brutalities, his unexpected gentlenesses, his furies of remorse; this man with the lofty brain, the perverted tastes, the weak, irresolute, indulgent heart, will never again be met with to the end of time; in all the endless combinations to come, this precise combination will never be found. Just as of all the faces the world will see, a face like the mask there will never again exchange glances with it. . . .

I looked at Corner, and saw his countenance once more aglow with the joy of a recovered Ideal; while Peschi's voice broke in on my reverie, speaking with the happy pride of the artist in a good and conscientious piece of work.

"Eh bien, how do you find it?" said he; "it is beautiful, is it not?"

GEORGE EGERTON

A Cross Line

The rather flat notes of a man's voice float out into the clear air, singing the refrain of a popular music-hall ditty. There is something incongruous between the melody and the surroundings. It seems profane, indelicate, to bring this slangy, vulgar tune, and with it the mental picture of footlight flare and fantastic dance, into the lovely freshness of this perfect spring day.

A woman sitting on a felled tree turns her head to meet its coming, and an expression flits across her face in which disgust and humorous appreciation are subtly blended. Her mind is nothing if not picturesque; her busy brain, with all its capabilities choked by a thousand vagrant fancies, is always producing pictures and finding associations between the most unlikely objects. She has been reading a little sketch written in the daintiest language of a fountain scene in Tanagra, and her vivid imagination has made it real to her. The slim, graceful maids grouped around it filling their exquisitely-formed earthen jars, the dainty poise of their classic heads, and the flowing folds of their draperies have been actually present with her; and now,—why, it is like the entrance of a half-typsy vagabond player bedizened in tawdry finery: the picture is blurred. She rests her head against the trunk of a pine-tree behind her, and awaits the singer. She is sitting on an incline in the midst of a wilderness of trees; some have blown down, some have been cut down, and the lopped branches lie about; moss and bracken and trailing bramble bushes, fir-cones, wild rose-bushes, and speckled red "fairy hats" fight for life in wild confusion. A disused quarry to the left is an ideal haunt of pike, and to the right a little river rushes along in haste to join a greater sister that is fighting a troubled way to the sea. A row of stepping-stones cross it, and if you were to stand on one you would see shoals of restless stone-loach "beardies" darting from side to side. The tails of several ducks can be seen above the water, and the paddle of their balancing feet and the gurgling suction of their bills as they search for larvae can be heard distinctly between the hum of insect, twitter of bird, and rustle of stream and leaf. The singer has changed his lay to a whistle, and presently he comes down the path a cool, neat, gray-clad figure, with a fishing creel slung across his back, and a trout rod held on his shoulder.

The air ceases abruptly, and his cold, gray eyes scan the seated figure with its gypsy ease of attitude, a scarlet shawl that has fallen from her shoulders forming an accentuative background to the slim roundness of her waist.

Persistent study, coupled with a varied experience of the female animal, has given the owner of the said gray eyes some facility in classing her, although it has not supplied him with any definite data as to what any one of the species may do in a given circumstance. To put it in his own words, in answer to a friend who chaffed him on his untiring pursuit of women as an interesting problem,—

"If a fellow has had much experience of his fellow-man he may divide him into types, and given a certain number of men and a certain number of circumstances, he is pretty safe on hitting on the line of action each type will strike. 'Taint so with woman. You may always look out for the unexpected; she generally upsets a fellow's calculations, and you are never safe in laying odds on her. Tell you what, old chappie, we may talk about superior intellect; but if a woman wasn't handicapped by her affection or need of it, the cleverest chap in Christendom would be just a bit of putty in her hands. I find them more fascinating as problems than anything going. Never let an opportunity slip to get new data—never!"

He did not now. He met the frank, unembarrassed gaze of eyes that would have looked with just the same bright inquiry at the advent of a hare or a toad, or any other object that might cross her path, and raised his hat with respectful courtesy, saying, in the drawling tone habitual with him,—

"I hope I am not trespassing?"

"I can't say; you may be; so may I, but no one has ever told me so!"

A pause. His quick glance has noted the thick wedding-ring on her slim brown hand and the flash of a diamond in its keeper. A lady decidedly. Fast?—perhaps. Original?—undoubtedly. Worth knowing?—rather.

"I am looking for a trout stream, but the directions I got were rather vague; might I—"

"It's straight ahead; but you won't catch anything now, at least not here,—sun's too glaring and water too low; a mile up you may in an hour's time."

"Oh, thanks awfully for the tip. You fish then?"

"Yes, sometimes."

"Trout run big here?" (What odd eyes the woman has! kind of magnetic.)

"No, seldom over a pound; but they are very game."

"Rare good sport, isn't it, whipping a stream? There is so much besides the mere catching of fish; the river and the trees and the quiet sets a fellow thinking; kind of sermon; makes a chap feel good, don't it?"

She smiles assentingly, and yet what the devil is she amused at, he queries mentally. An inspiration! he acts upon it, and says eagerly,—

"I wonder—I don't half like to ask, but fishing puts people on a common footing, don't it? You knowing the stream, you know, would you tell me what are the best flies to use?"

"I tie my own, but—"

"Do you? How clever of you! Wish I could;" and sitting down on the other end of the tree, he takes out his fly-book. "But I interrupted you, you were going to say—"

"Only,"—stretching out her hand, of a perfect shape but decidedly brown, for the book,—"that you might give the local fly-tyer a trial; he'll tell you. Later on, end of next month, or perhaps later, you might try the oak-fly,—the natural fly, you know. A horn is the best thing to hold them in, they get out of anything else; and put two on at a time."

"By Jove, I must try that dodge!"

He watches her as she handles his book and examines the contents critically, turning aside some with a glance, fingering others almost tenderly, holding them daintily, and noting the cock of wings and the hint of tinsel, with her head on one side,—a trick of hers, he thinks.

"Which do you like most, wet or dry fly?" She is looking at some dry flies.

"Oh," with that rare smile, "at the time I swear by whichever happens to catch most fish,—perhaps really dry fly. I fancy most of these flies are better for Scotland or England. Up to this, March-brown has been the most killing thing. But you might try an 'orange-grouse,'—that's always good here,—with perhaps a 'hare's ear' for a change, and put on a 'coachman' for the evenings. My husband [he steals a side look at her] brought home some beauties yesterday evening."

"Lucky fellow!"

She returns the book. There is a tone in his voice as he says this that jars on her, sensitive as she is to every inflection of a voice, with an intuition that is almost second sight. She gathers up her shawl,—she has a cream-colored woollen gown on, and her skin looks duskily foreign by contrast. She is on her feet before he can regain his, and says, with a cool little bend of her head: "Good afternoon, I wish you a full basket!"

Before he can raise his cap she is down the slope,

gliding with easy steps that have a strange grace, and then springing lightly from stone to stone across the stream. He feels small, snubbed someway; and he sits down on the spot where she sat, and lighting his pipe says, "Check!"

She is walking slowly up the garden path; a man in his shirt-sleeves is stooping among the tender young peas; a bundle of stakes lies next him, and he whistles softly and all out of tune as he twines the little tendrils round each new support. She looks at his broad shoulders and narrow flanks; his back is too long for great strength she thinks. He hears her step, and smiles up at her from under the shadow of his broad-leafed hat.

"How do you feel now, old woman?"

"Beastly! I've got that horrid qualmish feeling again. I can't get rid of it."

He has spread his coat on the side of the path, and pats it for her to sit down.

"What is it?" anxiously. "If you were a mare I'd know what to do for you. Have a nip of whiskey?"

He strides off without waiting for her reply, and comes back with it and a biscuit, kneels down and holds the glass to her lips. "Poor little woman, buck up! You'll see that'll fix you. Then you go, by-and-by, and have a shy at the fish."

She is about to say something, when a fresh qualm attacks her and she does not. He goes back to his tying.

"By Jove!" he says suddenly, "I forgot; got something to show you!"

After a few minutes he returns, carrying a basket covered with a piece of sacking; a dishevelled-looking hen, with spread wings trailing and her breast bare from sitting on her eggs, screeches after him. He puts it carefully down and uncovers it, disclosing seven little balls of yellow fluff splashed with olive-green; they look up sideways with bright round eyes, and their little spoon-bills look disproportionately large.

"Aren't they beauties?" enthusiastically. "This one is just out," taking up an egg; "mustn't let it get chilled; there is a chip out of it and a piece of hanging skin. Isn't it funny?" he asks, showing her how it is curled in the shell, with its paddles flattened and its bill breaking through the chip, and the slimy feathers sticking to its violet skin.

She suppresses an exclamation of disgust, and looks at his fresh-tinted skin instead. He is covering basket, hen, and all.

"How you love young things!" she says.

"Some! I had a filly once; she turned out a lovely

mare! I cried when I had to sell her; I wouldn't have let any one in God's world mount her."

"Yes, you would!"

"Who?" with a quick look of resentment.

"Me!"

"I wouldn't!"

"What! you wouldn't?"

"I wouldn't!"

"I think you would if I wanted to!" with a flash out of the tail of her eye.

"No, I wouldn't!"

"Then you would care more for her than for me. I would give you your choice," passionately, "her or me!"

"What nonsense!"

"Maybe," concentrated; "but it's lucky she isn't here to make deadly sense of it." A bumble-bee buzzes close to her ear, and she is roused to a sense of facts, and laughs to think how nearly they have quarrelled over a mare that was sold before she knew him.

Some evenings later she is stretched motionless in a chair; and yet she conveys an impression of restlessness,—a sensitively nervous person would feel it. She is gazing at her husband; her brows are drawn together, and make three little lines. He is reading, reading quietly, without moving his eyes quickly from side to side of the page as she does when she reads, and he pulls away at a big pipe with steady enjoyment. Her eyes turn from him to the window, and follow the course of two clouds; then they close for a few seconds, then open to watch him again. He looks up and smiles.

"Finished your book?"

There is a singular, soft monotony in his voice; the organ with which she replies is capable of more varied expression.

"Yes, it is a book makes one think. It would be a greater book if he were not an Englishman; he's afraid of shocking the big middle class. You wouldn't care about it."

"Finished your smoke?"

"No, it went out; too much fag to light up again! No," protestingly, "never you mind, old boy, why do you?"

He has drawn his long length out of his chair, and kneeling down beside her guards a lighted match from the incoming evening air. She draws in the smoke contentedly, and her eyes smile back with a general vague tenderness.

"Thank you, dear old man!"

"Going out again?" Negative head-shake.

"Back aching?" Affirmative nod, accompanied by

a steadily aimed puff of smoke, that she has been carefully inhaling, into his eyes.

"Scamp! Have your booties off?"

"Oh, don't you bother! Lizzie will do it."

He has seized a foot from under the rocker, and sitting on his heels holds it on his knee, while he unlaces the boot; then he loosens the stocking under her toes, and strokes her foot gently. "Now the other!" Then he drops both boots outside the door, and fetching a little pair of slippers, past their first smartness, from the bedroom, puts one on. He examines the left foot: it is a little swollen round the ankle, and he presses his broad fingers gently round it as one sees a man do to a horse with windgalls. Then he pulls the rocker nearer to his chair, and rests the slipperless foot on his thigh. He relights his pipe, takes up his book, and rubs softly from ankle to toes as he reads.

She smokes, and watches him, diverting herself by imagining him in the hats of different periods. His is a delicate skinned face, with regular features; the eyes are fine in color and shape, with the luminous clearness of a child's; his pointed beard is soft and curly. She looks at his hand,—a broad, strong hand with capable fingers; the hand of a craftsman, a contradiction to the face with its distinguished delicacy. She holds her own up, with a cigarette poised between the first and second fingers, idly pleased with its beauty of form and delicate, nervous slightness. One speculation chases the other in her quick brain: odd questions as to race arise; she dives into theories as to the why and wherefore of their distinctive natures, and holds a mental debate in which she takes both sides of the question impartially. He has finished his pipe, laid down his book, and is gazing dreamily into space, with his eyes darkened by their long lashes and a look of tender melancholy in their clear depths.

"What are you thinking of?" There is a look of expectation in her quivering nervous little face.

He turns to her, chafing her ankle again. "I was wondering if lob-worms would do for—"

He stops: a strange look of disappointment flits across her face and is lost in an hysterical peal of laughter.

"You are the best emotional check I ever knew," she gasps.

He stares at her in utter bewilderment, and then a slow smile creeps to his eyes and curves the thin lips under his mustache,—a smile at her. "You seem amused, Gypsy!"

She springs out of her chair, and takes book and pipe; he follows the latter anxiously with his eyes until he sees it laid safely on the table. Then she perches herself, resting her knees against one of his legs, while she hooks her feet back under the other.

"Now I am all up, don't I look small?"

He smiles his slow smile. "Yes, I believe you are made of gutta percha."

She is stroking out all the lines in his face with the tip of her finger; then she runs it through his hair. He twists his head half impatiently; she desists.

"I divide all the people in the world," she says, "into those who like their hair played with, and those who don't. Having my hair brushed gives me more pleasure than anything else; it's delicious. I'd *purr* if I knew how. I notice," meditatively, "I am never in sympathy with those who don't like it. I am with those who do; I always get on with them."

"You are a queer little devil!"

"Am I? I shouldn't have thought you would have found out I was the latter at all. I wish I were a man! I believe if I were a man, I'd be a disgrace to my family."

"Why?"

"I'd go on a jolly old spree!"

He laughs: "Poor little woman! is it so dull?" There is a gleam of deviltry in her eyes, and she whispers solemnly,—

"Begin with a D," and she traces imaginary letters across his forehead, and ending with a flick over his ear, says, "and that is the tail of the y!" After a short silence she queries: "Are you fond of me?" She is rubbing her chin up and down his face.

"Of course I am, don't you know it?"

"Yes, perhaps I do," impatiently; "but I want to be told it. A woman doesn't care a fig for a love as deep as the death-sea and as silent; she wants something that tells her it in little waves all the time. It isn't the *love*, you know, it's the *being loved*; it isn't really the *man*, it's his *loving!*"

"By Jove, you're a rum un!"

"I wish I wasn't, then. I wish I was as commonplace as—You don't tell me anything about myself," a fierce little kiss; "you might, even if it were lies. Other men who cared for me told me things about my eyes, my hands, anything. I don't believe you notice."

"Yes I *do*, little one, only I think it."

"Yes, but I don't care a bit for your thinking; if I can't see what's in your head, what good is it to me?"

"I wish I could understand you, dear!"

"I wish to God you could! Perhaps if you were badder and I were gooder we'd meet halfway. *You* are an awfully good old chap; it's just men like you send women like me to the devil!"

"But you are good," kissing her,—"a real good chum! You understand a fellow's weak points; you don't blow him up if he gets on a bit. Why," enthusiastically, "being married to you is like chumming with a chap! Why," admiringly, "do you remember before we were married, when I let that card fall out of my pocket? Why, I couldn't have told another girl about her! she wouldn't have believed that I *was* straight; she'd have thrown me over, and you sent her a quid because she was sick. You are a great little woman!"

"Don't see it!" she is biting his ear. "Perhaps I was a man last time, and some hereditary memories are cropping up in this incarnation!"

He looks so utterly at sea that she must laugh again, and, kneeling up, shuts his eyes with kisses, and bites his chin and shakes it like a terrier in her strong little teeth.

"You imp! was there ever such a woman!"

Catching her wrists, he parts his knees and drops her on to the rug; then perhaps the subtle magnetism that is in her affects him, for he stoops and snatches her up and carries her up and down, and then over to the window, and lets the fading light with its glimmer of moonshine play on her odd face with its tantalizing changes, and his eyes dilate and his color deepens as he crushes her soft little body to him and carries her off to her room.

★

Summer is waning, and the harvest is ripe for ingathering, and the voice of the reaping machine is loud in the land. She is stretched on her back on the short, heather-mixed moss at the side of a bog stream. Rod and creel are flung aside, and the wanton breeze with the breath of coolness it has gathered in its passage over the murky dykes of black bog-water is playing with the tail-fly, tossing it to and fro with a half threat to fasten it to a prickly spine of golden gorse. Bunches of bog-wool nod their fluffy heads, and through the myriad indefinite sounds comes the regular scrape of a strickle on the scythe of a reaper in a neighboring meadow. Overhead a flotilla of clouds is steering from the south in a northeasterly direction. Her eyes follow them,— old-time galleons, she thinks, with their wealth of snowy sail spread, riding breast to breast up a wide, blue fjord after victory. The sails of the last are rose-flushed, with a silver edge. Someway she thinks of Cleopatra sailing down to meet Antony, and a great longing fills her soul to sail off somewhere too,— away from the daily need of dinner-getting and the recurring Monday with its washing, life with its tame duties and virtuous monotony. She fancies herself in Arabia on the back of a swift steed; flashing eyes set in dark faces surround her, and she can see the clouds of sand swirl, and feel the swing under her of

A Cross Line

his rushing stride; and her thoughts shape themselves into a wild song,—a song to her steed of flowing mane and satin skin, an uncouth rhythmical jingle with a feverish beat; a song to the untamed spirit that dwells in her. Then she fancies she is on the stage of an ancient theatre, out in the open air, with hundreds of faces upturned toward her. She is gauze-clad in a cobweb garment of wondrous tissue; her arms are clasped by jewelled snakes, and one with quivering diamond fangs coils round her hips; her hair floats loosely, and her feet are sandal-clad, and the delicate breath of vines and the salt freshness of an incoming sea seem to fill her nostrils. She bounds forward and dances, bends her lissome waist, and curves her slender arms, and gives to the soul of each man what he craves, be it good or evil. And she can feel now, lying here in the shade of Irish hills, with her head resting on her scarlet shawl and her eyes closed, the grand, intoxicating power of swaying all these human souls to wonder and applause. She can see herself with parted lips and panting, rounded breasts, and a dancing devil in each glowing eye, sway voluptuously to the wild music that rises, now slow, now fast, now deliriously wild, seductive, intoxicating, with a human note of passion in its strain. She can feel the answering shiver of emotion that quivers up to her from the dense audience, spellbound by the motion of her glancing feet; and she flies swifter and swifter, and lighter and lighter, till the very serpents seem alive with jewelled scintillations. One quivering, gleaming, daring bound, and she stands with outstretched arms and passion-filled eyes, poised on one slender foot, asking a supreme note to finish her dream of motion; and the men rise to a man and answer her, and cheer, cheer till the echoes shout from the surrounding hills and tumble wildly down the crags.

The clouds have sailed away, leaving long feathery streaks in their wake. Her eyes have an inseeing look, and she is tremulous with excitement; she can hear yet that last grand shout, and the strain of that old-time music that she has never heard in this life of hers, save as an inner accompaniment to the memory of hidden things, born with her, not of this time.

And her thoughts go to other women she has known, women good and bad, school friends, casual acquaintances, women workers,—joyless machines for grinding daily corn, unwilling maids grown old in the endeavor to get settled, patient wives who bear little ones to indifferent husbands until they wear out,—a long array. She busies herself with questioning. Have they, too, this thirst for excitement, for change, this restless craving for sun and love and motion? Stray words, half confidences, glimpses through soul-chinks of suppressed fires, actual outbreaks, domestic catastrophes,—how the ghosts dance in the cells of her memory! And she laughs, laughs softly to herself, because the denseness of man, his chivalrous, conservative devotion to the female idea he has created, blinds him, perhaps happily, to the problems of her complex nature. "Ay," she mutters musingly, "the wisest of them can only say we are enigmas; each one of them sets about solving the riddle of the *ewig weibliche*,—and well it is that the workings of our hearts are closed to them, that we are cunning enough or *great* enough to seem to be what they would have us, rather than be what we are. But few of them have had the insight to find out the key to our seeming contradictions,—the why a refined, physically fragile woman will mate with a brute, a mere male animal with primitive passions, and love him; the why strength and beauty appeal more often than the more subtly fine qualities of mind or heart; the why women (and not the innocent ones) will condone sins that men find hard to forgive in their fellows. They have all overlooked the eternal wildness, the untamed primitive savage temperament that lurks in the mildest, best woman. Deep in through ages of convention this primeval trait burns,—an untamable quality that may be concealed but is never eradicated by culture, the keynote of woman's witchcraft and woman's strength. But it is there, sure enough, and each woman is conscious of it in her truth-telling hours of quiet self-scrutiny; and each woman in God's wide world will deny it, and each woman will help another to conceal it,—for the woman who tells the truth and is not a liar about these things is untrue to her sex and abhorrent to man, for he has fashioned a model on imaginary lines, and he has said, 'So I would have you!' and every woman is an unconscious liar, for so man loves her. And when a Strindberg or a Nietzsche arises and peers into the recesses of her nature and dissects her ruthlessly, the men shriek out louder than the women, because the truth is at all times unpalatable, and the gods they have set up are dear to them—"

"Dreaming, or speering into futurity? You have the look of a seer. I believe you are half a witch!" And he drops his gray-clad figure on the turf; he has dropped his drawl long ago in midsummer.

"Is not every woman that? Let us hope I'm for my friends a white one."

"A-ah! Have you many friends?"

"That is a query! If you mean many correspondents, many persons who send me Christmas cards, or remember my birthday, or figure in my address book,—no."

"Well, grant I don't mean that!"

"Well, perhaps, yes. Scattered over the world, if my death were belled out, many women would give me a tear, and some a prayer; and many men would turn back a page in their memory and give me a kind thought, perhaps a regret, and go back to their work with a feeling of having lost something that they never possessed. I am a creature of moments. Women have told me that I came into their lives just when they needed me; men had no need to tell me, I felt it. People have needed me more than I them. I have given freely whatever they craved from me in the way of understanding or love; I have touched sore places they showed me, and healed them,—but they never got at me. I have been for myself, and helped myself, and borne the burden of my own mistakes. Some have chafed at my self-sufficiency, and have called me fickle,—not understanding that they gave me nothing, and that when I had served them their moment was ended, and I was to pass on. I read people easily, I am written in black letter to most—"

"To your husband?"

"He," quickly,—"we will not speak of him; it is not loyal."

"Do not I understand you a little?"

"You do not misunderstand me."

"That is something."

"It is much!"

"Is it?" searching her face. "It is not one grain of sand in the desert that stretches between you and me, and you are as impenetrable as a sphinx at the end of it. This," passionately, "is my moment, and what have you given me?"

"Perhaps less than other men I have known; but you want less. You are a little like me,—you can stand alone; and yet," her voice is shaking, "have I given you nothing?"

He laughs, and she winces; and they sit silent, and they both feel as if the earth between them is laid with infinitesimal electric threads vibrating with a common pain. Her eyes are filled with tears that burn but don't fall; and she can see his some way through her closed lids, see their cool grayness troubled by sudden fire, and she rolls her handkerchief into a moist cambric ball between her cold palms.

"You have given me something, something to carry away with me,—an infernal want. You ought to be satisfied: I am infernally miserable. You," nearer, "have the most tantalizing mouth in the world when your lips tremble like that. I—What! can you cry? You?"

"Yes, even I can cry!"

"You dear woman!" pause; "and I can't help you?"

"You can't help me; no man can. Don't think it is because you are you I cry, but because you probe a little nearer into the real me that I feel so."

"Was it necessary to say that?" reproachfully; "do you think I don't know it? I can't for the life of me think how you, with that free gypsy nature of yours, could bind yourself to a monotonous country life, with no excitement, no change. I wish I could offer you my yacht; do you like the sea?"

"I love it; it answers one's moods."

"Well, let us play pretending, as the children say. Grant that I could, I would hang your cabin with your own colors, fill it with books (all those I have heard you say you care for), make it a nest as rare as the bird it would shelter. You would reign supreme. When your highness would deign to honor her servant, I would come and humor your every whim. If you were glad, you could clap your hands and order music, and we would dance on the white deck, and we would skim through the sunshine of Southern seas on a spice-scented breeze. You make me poetical. And if you were angry, you could vent your feelings on me, and I would give in and bow my head to your mood. And we would drop anchor, and stroll through strange cities,—go far inland and glean folklore out of the beaten track of everyday tourists; and at night, when the harbor slept, we would sail out through the moonlight over silver seas. You are smiling,—you look so different when you smile; do you like my picture?"

"Some of it!"

"What not?"

"You!"

"Thank you."

"You asked me. Can't you understand where the spell lies? It is the freedom, the freshness, the vague danger, the unknown that has a witchery for me,— ay, for every woman!"

"Are you incapable of affection, then?"

"Of course not. I share," bitterly, "that crowning disability of my sex; but not willingly,—I chafe under it. My God! if it were not for that, we women would master the world! I tell you, men would be no match for us! At heart we care nothing for laws, nothing for systems; all your elaborately reasoned codes for controlling morals or man do not weigh a jot with us against an impulse, an instinct. We learn those things from you,—you tamed, amenable animals; they are not natural to us. It is a wise disposition of Providence that this untamableness of ours is corrected by our affections. We forge our own chains in a moment of softness, and then," bitterly, "we may as well wear them with a good grace. Perhaps many of our seeming contradictions are only the outward evidences of inward chafing. Bah! the qualities that go to make a Napoleon—superstition, want of honor, disregard of opinion, and the eternal I—are oftener to be found in a woman than a man. Lucky for the world, perhaps, that all these attributes weigh as nothing in the balance with the need to love, if she be a good woman; to be loved, if she is of a coarser fibre."

"I never met any one like you; you are a strange woman!"

"No, I am merely a truthful one. Women talk to me—why? I can't say; but always they come, strip their hearts and souls naked, and let me see the hidden folds of their natures. The greatest tragedies I have ever read are child's play to those I have seen acted in the inner life of outwardly commonplace women. A woman must beware of speaking the truth to a man; he loves her the less for it. It is the elusive spirit in her, that he divines but cannot seize, that facinates and keeps him."

There is a long silence; the sun is waning and the scythes are silent, and overhead the crows are circling,—a croaking, irregular army, homeward bound from a long day's pillage.

She has made no sign, yet so subtilely is the air charged with her that he feels but a few moments remain to him. He goes over and kneels beside her, and fixes his eyes on her odd, dark face. They both tremble, yet neither speaks. His breath is coming quickly, and the bistre stains about her eyes seem to have deepened, perhaps by contrast, as she has paled.

"Look at me!"

She turns her head right round and gazes straight into his face; a few drops of sweat glisten on his forehead.

"You witch woman! what am I to do with myself? Is my moment ended?"

"I think so."

"Lord, what a mouth!"

"Don't! oh, don't!"

"No, I won't. But do you mean it? Am I, who understand your every mood, your restless spirit, to vanish out of your life? You can't mean it! Listen!—are you listening to me? I can't see your face; take down your hands. Go back over every chance meeting you and I have had together since I met you first by the river, and judge them fairly. To-day is Monday: Wednesday afternoon I shall pass your gate, and if—if my moment is ended, and you mean to send me away, to let me go with this weary aching—"

"A-ah!" she stretches out one brown hand appealingly, but he does not touch it.

"Hang something white on the lilac bush!"

She gathers up creel and rod, and he takes her shawl, and wrapping it round her holds her a moment in it, and looks searchingly into her eyes, then stands back and raises his hat, and she glides away through the reedy grass.

Wednesday morning she lies watching the clouds sail by. A late rose-spray nods into the open window, and the petals fall every time. A big bee buzzes in and fills the room with his bass note, and then dances out again. She can hear his footstep on the gravel. Presently he looks in over the half window,—

"Get up and come out,—'twill do you good; have a brisk walk!"

She shakes her head languidly, and he throws a great soft, dewy rose with sure aim on her breast.

"Shall I go in and lift you out and put you, 'nighty' and all, into your tub?"

"No!" impatiently. "I'll get up just now."

The head disappears, and she rises wearily and gets through her dressing slowly, stopped every moment by a feeling of faintness. He finds her presently rocking slowly to and fro with closed eyes, and drops a leaf with three plums in it on to her lap.

"I have been watching four for the last week, but a bird, greedy beggar, got one this morning early: try them. Don't you mind, old girl, I'll pour out my own tea!"

She bites into one and tries to finish it, but cannot. "You are a good old man!" she says, and the tears come unbidden to her eyes, and trickle down her cheeks, dropping on to the plums, streaking their delicate bloom.

He looks uneasily at her, but doesn't know what to do; and when he has finished his breakfast he stoops over her chair and strokes her hair, saying, as he leaves a kiss on the top of her head, "Come out into the air, little woman; do you a world of good!"

And presently she hears the sharp thrust of his spade above the bee's hum, leaf rustle, and the myriad late summer sounds that thrill through the air. It irritates her almost to screaming point; there is a practical non-sympathy about it; she can distinguish the regular one, two, three, the thrust, interval, then pat, pat, on the upturned sod. To-day she wants some one, and her thoughts wander to, and she wonders what, the gray-eyed man who never misunderstands her, would say to her. Oh, she wants some one so badly to soothe her; and she yearns for the little mother who is twenty years under the daisies,—the little mother who is a faint memory strengthened by a daguerreotype in which she sits with silk-mittened hands primly crossed on the lap of her moiré gown, a diamond brooch fastening the black-velvet ribbon crossed so stiffly over her lace collar, the shining tender eyes looking steadily out, and her hair in the fashion of fifty-six. How that spade dominates over every sound! and what a sickening pain she has, an odd pain; she never felt it before. Supposing she were to die, she tries to fancy how she would look; they would be sure to plaster her curls down. He might be digging her grave—no, it is the patch where the early peas grew, the peas that were eaten with the twelve weeks' ducklings: she remembers them, little fluffy golden balls with waxen bills, and such dainty paddles,—remembers holding an egg to her ear and listening to it cheep inside before even there was a chip in the shell. Strange how things come to life! What! she sits bolt upright and holds tightly to the chair, and a questioning, awesome look comes over her face; and then the quick blood creeps up through her olive skin right up to her temples, and she buries her face in her hands and sits so a long time.

The maid comes in and watches her curiously, and moves softly about. The look in her eyes is the look of a faithful dog, and she loves her with the same rare fidelity. She hesitates, then goes into the bedroom and stands thoughtfully, with her hands clasped over her breast. She is a tall, thin, flat-waisted woman, with misty blue eyes and a receding chin. Her hair is pretty. She turns as her mistress comes in, with an expectant look on her face. She has taken up a nightgown, but holds it idly.

"Lizzie, had you ever a child?"

The girl's long left hand is ringless; yet she asks it with a quiet insistence, as if she knew what the answer would be, and her odd eyes read her face with an almost cruel steadiness. The girl flushes painfully, and then whitens; her very eyes seem to pale, and her under lip twitches as she jerks out huskily,—

"Yes!"

"What happened to it?"

"It died, M'am."

"Poor thing! Poor old Liz!"

She pats the girl's hand softly, and the latter stands dumbly and looks down at both hands, as if fearful to break the wonder of a caress. She whispers hesitatingly,—

"Have you—have you any little things left?"

And she laughs such a soft, cooing little laugh, like the chirring of a ring-dove, and nods shyly back in reply to the tall maid's questioning look. The latter goes out, and comes back with a flat, red-painted deal box, and unlocks it. It does not hold very much, and the tiny garments are not of costly material; but the two women pore over them as a gem collector over a rare stone. She has a glimpse of thick-crested paper as the girl unties a packet of letters, and looks away until she says tenderly,—

"Look, M'am!"

A little bit of hair inside a paper heart. It is almost white, so silky and so fine that it is more like a thread of bog-wool than a baby's hair; and the mistress, who is a wife, puts her arms round the tall maid, who has never had more than a moral claim to the name, and kisses her in her quick way.

The afternoon is drawing on; she is kneeling before an open trunk, with flushed cheeks and sparkling eyes. A heap of unused, dainty lace-trimmed ribbon-decked cambric garments are scattered around her. She holds the soft, scented web to her cheek and smiles musingly; and then she rouses herself and sets to work, sorting out the finest, with the narrowest lace and tiniest ribbon, and puckers her swarthy brows, and measures lengths along her middle finger, and then gets slowly up, as if careful of herself as a precious thing, and half afraid.

"Lizzie!"

"Yes, M'am!"

"Wasn't it lucky they were too fine for every day? They will be so pretty. Look at this one with the tiny valenciennes edging. Why, one nightgown will make a dozen little shirts,—such elfin-shirts as they are too; and Lizzie!"

"Yes, M'am!"

"Just hang it out on the lilac-bush,—mind, the lilac-bush!"

"Yes, M'am!"

"Or, Lizzie, wait: I'll do it myself!"

Kate Chopin

An Egyptian Cigarette

My friend, the Architect, who is something of a traveler, was showing us various curios which he had gathered during a visit to the Orient.

"Here is something for you," he said, picking up a small box and turning it over in his hand. "You are a cigarette-smoker; take this home with you. It was given to me in Cairo by a species of fakir, who fancied I had done him a good turn."

The box was covered with glazed, yellow paper, so skillfully gummed as to appear to be all one piece. It bore no label, no stamp—nothing to indicate its contents.

"How do you know they are cigarettes?" I asked, taking the box and turning it stupidly around as one turns a sealed letter and speculates before opening it.

"I only know what he told me," replied the Architect, "but it is easy enough to determine the question of his integrity." He handed me a sharp, pointed paper-cutter, and with it I opened the lid as carefully as possible.

The box contained six cigarettes, evidently handmade. The wrappers were of pale-yellow paper, and the tobacco was almost the same color. It was of finer cut than the Turkish or ordinary Egyptian, and threads of it stuck out at either end.

"Will you try one now, Madam?" asked the Architect, offering to strike a match.

"Not now and not here," I replied, "after the coffee, if you will permit me to slip into your smoking-den. Some of the women here detest the odor of cigarettes."

The smoking-room lay at the end of a short, curved passage. Its appointments were exclusively Oriental. A broad, low window opened out upon a balcony that overhung the garden. From the divan upon which I reclined, only the swaying tree-tops could be seen. The maple leaves glistened in the afternoon sun. Beside the divan was a low stand which contained the complete paraphernalia of a smoker. I was feeling quite comfortable, and congratulated myself upon having escaped for a while the incessant chatter of the women that reached me faintly.

I took a cigarette and lit it, placing the box upon

the stand just as the tiny clock, which was there, chimed in silvery strokes the hour of five.

I took one long inspiration of the Egyptian cigarette. The gray-green smoke arose in a small puffy column that spread and broadened, that seemed to fill the room. I could see the maple leaves dimly, as if they were veiled in a shimmer of moonlight. A subtle, disturbing current passed through my whole body and went to my head like the fumes of disturbing wine. I took another deep inhalation of the cigarette.

"Ah! the sand has blistered my cheek! I have lain here all day with my face in the sand. To-night, when the everlasting stars are burning, I shall drag myself to the river."

He will never come back.

Thus far I followed him; with flying feet; with stumbling feet; with hands and knees, crawling; and outstretched arms, and here I have fallen in the sand.

The sand has blistered my cheek; it has blistered all my body, and the sun is crushing me with hot torture. There is shade beneath yonder cluster of palms.

I shall stay here in the sand till the hour and the night comes.

I laughed at the oracles and scoffed at the stars when they told that after the rapture of life I would open my arms inviting death, and the waters would envelop me.

Oh! how the sand blisters my cheek! and I have no tears to quench the fire. The river is cool and the night is not far distant.

I turned from the gods and said: "There is but one; Bardja is my god." That was when I decked myself with lilies and wove flowers into a garland and held him close in the frail, sweet fetters.

He will never come back. He turned upon his camel as he rode away. He turned and looked at me crouching here and laughed, showing his gleaming white teeth.

Whenever he kissed me and went away he always came back again. Whenever he flamed with fierce anger and left me with stinging words, he always came back. But to-day he neither kissed me nor was he angry. He only said:

"Oh! I am tired of fetters, and kisses, and you. I am going away. You will never see me again. I am going to the great city where men swarm like bees. I am going beyond, where the monster stones are rising heavenward in a monument for the

An Egyptian Cigarette

unborn ages. Oh! I am tired. You will see me no more."

And he rode away on his camel. He smiled and showed his cruel white teeth as he turned to look at me crouching here.

How slow the hours drag! It seems to me that I have lain here for days in the sand, feeding upon despair. Despair is bitter and it nourishes resolve.

I hear the wings of a bird flapping above my head, flying low, in circles.

The sun is gone.

The sand has crept between my lips and teeth and under my parched tongue.

If I raise my head, perhaps I shall see the evening star.

Oh! the pain in my arms and legs! My body is sore and bruised as if broken. Why can I not rise and run as I did this morning? Why must I drag myself thus like a wounded serpent, twisting and writhing?

The river is near at hand. I hear it—I see it—Oh! the sand! Oh! the shine! How cool! how cold!

The water! the water! In my eyes, my ears, my throat! It strangles me! Help! will the gods not help me?

Oh! the sweet rapture of rest! There is music in

the Temple. And here is fruit to taste. Bardja came with the music—The moon shines and the breeze is soft—A garland of flowers—let us go into the King's garden and look at the blue lily, Bardja.

The maple leaves looked as if a silvery shimmer enveloped them. The gray-green smoke no longer filled the room. I could hardly lift the lids of my eyes. The weight of centuries seemed to suffocate my soul that struggled to escape, to free itself and breathe.

I had tasted the depths of human despair.

The little clock upon the stand pointed to a quarter past five. The cigarettes still reposed in the yellow box. Only the stub of the one I had smoked remained. I had laid it in the ash tray.

As I looked at the cigarettes in their pale wrappers, I wondered what other visions they might hold for me; what might I not find in their mystic fumes? Perhaps a vision of celestial peace; a dream of hopes fulfilled; a taste of rapture, such as had not entered into my mind to conceive.

I took the cigarettes and crumpled them between my hands. I walked to the window and spread my palms wide. The light breeze caught up the golden threads and bore them writhing and dancing far out among the maple leaves.

An Egyptian Cigarette

My friend, the Architect, lifted the curtain and entered, bringing me a second cup of coffee.

"How pale you are!" he exclaimed, solicitously. "Are you not feeling well?"

"A little the worse for a dream," I told him.

Max Beerbohm

Enoch Soames
A Memory of the Eighteen-Nineties

When a book about the literature of the eighteen-nineties was given by Mr. Holbrook Jackson to the world, I looked eagerly in the index for Soames, Enoch. It was as I feared: he was not there. But everybody else was. Many writers whom I had quite forgotten, or remembered but faintly, lived again for me, they and their work, in Mr. Holbrook Jackson's pages. The book was as thorough as it was brilliantly written. And thus the omission found by me was an all the deadlier record of poor Soames's failure to impress himself on his decade.

I dare say I am the only person who noticed the omission. Soames had failed so piteously as all that! Nor is there a counterpoise in the thought that if he had had some measure of success he might have passed, like those others, out of my mind, to return only at the historian's beck. It is true that had his gifts, such as they were, been acknowledged in his lifetime, he would never have made the bargain I saw him make—that strange bargain whose results have kept him always in the foreground of my memory. But it is from those very results that the full piteousness of him glares out.

Now my compassion, however, impels me to write of him. For his sake, poor fellow, I should be inclined to keep my pen out of the ink. It is ill to deride the dead. And how can I write about Enoch Soames without making him ridiculous? Or, rather, how am I to hush up the horrid fact that he *was* ridiculous? I shall not be able to do that. Yet, sooner or later, write about him I must. You will see in due course that I have no option. And I may as well get the thing done now.

In the summer term of '93 a bolt from the blue flashed down on Oxford. It drove deep; it hurtlingly embedded itself in the soil. Dons and undergraduates stood around, rather pale, discussing nothing but it. Whence came it, this meteorite? From Paris. Its name? Will Rothenstein. Its aim? To do a series of twenty-four portraits in lithograph. These were to be published from the Bodley Head, London. The matter was urgent. Already the warden of A, and the master of B, and the Regius Professor of C had meekly "sat." Dignified and doddering old men who had never consented to sit to any one could not withstand this dynamic little stranger. He did not sue; he invited: he did not invite; he commanded. He was twenty-one years old. He wore spectacles that flashed more than any other pair ever seen. He was a wit. He was brimful of ideas. He knew Whistler. He knew Daudet and the Goncourts. He knew every one in Paris. He knew them all by heart. He was Paris in Oxford. It was whispered that, so soon as he had polished off his selection of dons, he was going to include a few undergraduates. It was a proud day for me when I—I was included. I liked Rothenstein not less than I feared him; and there arose between us a friendship that has grown ever warmer, and been more and more valued by me, with every passing year.

At the end of term he settled in, or, rather, meteoritically into, London. It was to him I owed my first knowledge of that forever-enchanting little world-in-itself, Chelsea, and my first acquaintance with Walter Sickert and other august elders who dwelt there. It was Rothenstein that took me to see, in Cambridge Street, Pimlico, a young man whose drawings were already famous among the few—Aubrey Beardsley by name. With Rothenstein I paid my first visit to the Bodley Head. By him I was inducted into another haunt of intellect and daring, the domino-room of the Café Royal.

There, on that October evening—there, in that exuberant vista of gilding and crimson velvet set amidst all those opposing mirrors and upholding caryatids, with fumes of tobacco ever rising to the painted and pagan ceiling, and with the hum of presumably cynical conversation broken into so sharply now and again by the clatter of dominoes shuffled on marble tables, I drew a deep breath and, "This indeed," said I to myself, "is life!" (Forgive me that theory. Remember the waging of even the South African War was not yet.)

It was the hour before dinner. We drank vermouth. Those who knew Rothenstein were pointing him out to those who knew him only by name. Men were constantly coming in through the swing-doors and wandering slowly up and down in search of vacant tables or of tables occupied by friends. One of these rovers interested me because I was sure he wanted to catch Rothenstein's eye. He had twice passed our table, with a hesitating look; but Rothenstein, in the thick of a disquisition on Puvis de Chavannes, had not seen him. He was a stooping, shambling person, rather tall, very pale, with longish and brownish hair. He had a thin, vague beard, or, rather, he had a chin on which a large number of hairs weakly curled and clustered to cover its retreat. He was an odd-looking person; but in the nineties odd apparitions were more frequent, I think, than they are now. The young writers of that era—and I was sure this man was a writer—strove earnestly to be distinct in aspect. This man had striven unsuccessfully. He wore a soft black hat of clerical kind, but of Bohemian intention, and a gray waterproof cape which, perhaps because it was waterproof, failed to be romantic. I decided that "dim" was the *mot juste* for him. I had already essayed to write, and was immensely keen on the *mot juste*, that Holy Grail of the period.

The dim man was now again approaching our table, and this time he made up his mind to pause in front of it.

"You don't remember me," he said in a toneless voice.

Rothenstein brightly focused him.

"Yes, I do," he replied after a moment, with pride rather than effusion—pride in a retentive memory. "Edwin Soames."

"Enoch Soames," said Enoch.

"Enoch Soames," repeated Rothenstein in a tone implying that it was enough to have hit on the surname. "We met in Paris a few times when you were living there. We met at the Café Groche."

"And I came to your studio once."

"Oh, yes; I was sorry I was out."

"But you were in. You showed me some of your paintings, you know. I hear you're in Chelsea now."

"Yes."

I almost wondered that Mr. Soames did not, after this monosyllable, pass along. He stood patiently there, rather like a dumb animal, rather like a donkey looking over a gate. A sad figure, his. It occurred to me that "hungry" was perhaps the *mot juste* for him; but—hungry for what? He looked as if he had little appetite for anything. I was sorry for him; and Rothenstein, though he had not invited him to Chelsea, did ask him to sit down and have something to drink.

Seated, he was more self-assertive. He flung back the wings of his cape with a gesture which, had not those wings been waterproof, might have seemed to hurl defiance at things in general. And he ordered an absinthe. "*Je me tiens toujours fidèle,*" he told Rothenstein, "*à la sorcière glauque.*"

"It is bad for you," said Rothenstein, dryly.

"Nothing is bad for one," answered Soames. "*Dans ce monde il n'y a ni bien ni mal.*"

"Nothing good and nothing bad? How do you mean?"

"I explained it all in the preface to 'Negations.'"

"'Negations'?"

"Yes, I gave you a copy of it."

"Oh, yes, of course. But did you explain, for instance, that there was no such thing as bad or good grammar?"

"N-no," said Soames. "Of course in art there is the good and the evil. But in life—no." He was rolling a cigarette. He had weak, white hands, not well washed, and with finger-tips much stained with nicotine. "In life there are illusions of good and evil, but"—his voice trailed away to a murmur in which the words "*vieux jeu*" and "rococo" were faintly audible. I think he felt he was not doing himself justice, and feared that Rothenstein was going to point out fallacies. Anyhow, he cleared his throat and said, "*Parlons d'autre chose.*"

It occurs to you that he was a fool? It didn't to me. I was young, and had not the clarity of judgment that Rothenstein already had. Soames was quite five or six years older than either of us. Also— he had written a book. It was wonderful to have written a book.

If Rothenstein had not been there, I should have revered Soames. Even as it was, I respected him. And I was very near indeed to reverence when he said he had another book coming out soon. I asked if I might ask what kind of book it was to be.

"My poems," he answered. Rothenstein asked if this was to be the title of the book. The poet meditated on this suggestion, but said he rather thought of giving the book no title at all. "If a book is good in itself—" he murmured, and waved his cigarette.

Rothenstein objected that absence of title might be bad for the sale of a book.

"If," he urged, "I went into a bookseller's and said simply, 'Have you got?' or, 'Have you a copy of?' how would they know what I wanted?"

"Oh, of course I should have my name on the cover," Soames answered earnestly. "And I rather want," he added, looking hard at Rothenstein, "to have a drawing of myself as frontispiece." Rothenstein admitted that this was a capital idea, and mentioned that he was going into the country and would be there for some time. He then looked at his watch, exclaimed at the hour, paid the waiter, and went away with me to dinner. Soames remained at his post of fidelity to the glaucous witch.

"Why were you so determined not to draw him?" I asked.

"Draw him? Him? How can one draw a man who doesn't exist?"

"He is dim," I admitted. But my *mot juste* fell flat. Rothenstein repeated that Soames was non-existent.

Enoch Soames

Still, Soames had written a book. I asked if Rothenstein had read "Negations." He said he had looked into it, "but," he added crisply, "I don't profess to know anything about writing." A reservation very characteristic of the period! Painters would not then allow that any one outside their own order had a right to any opinion about painting. This law (graven on the tablets brought down by Whistler from the summit of Fuji-yama) imposed certain limitations. If other arts than painting were not utterly unintelligible to all but the men who practised them, the law tottered—the Monroe Doctrine, as it were, did not hold good. Therefore no painter would offer an opinion of a book without warning you at any rate that his opinion was worthless. No one is a better judge of literature than Rothenstein; but it wouldn't have done to tell him so in those days, and I knew that I must form an unaided judgment of "Negations."

Not to buy a book of which I had met the author face to face would have been for me in those days an impossible act of self-denial. When I returned to Oxford for the Christmas term I had duly secured "Negations." I used to keep it lying carelessly on the table in my room, and whenever a friend took it up and asked what it was about, I would say: "Oh, it's rather a remarkable book. It's by a man whom I know." Just "what it was about" I never was able to say. Head or tail was just what I hadn't made of that slim, green volume. I found in the preface no clue to the labyrinth of contents, and in that labyrinth nothing to explain the preface.

> Lean near to life. Lean very near—nearer.
> Life is well and therein nor warp nor woof is, but web only.
> It is for this I am Catholick in church and in thought, yet do let swift Mood weave there what the shuttle of Mood wills.

These were the opening phrases of the preface, but those which followed were less easy to understand. Then came "Stark: *A Conte*," about a *midinette* who, so far as I could gather, murdered, or was about to murder, a *mannequin*. It was rather like a story by Catulle Mendès in which the translator had either skipped or cut out every alternate sentence. Next, a dialogue between Pan and St. Ursula, lacking, I rather thought, in "snap." Next, some aphorisms (entitled ἀφορίσματα). Throughout, in fact, there was a great variety of form, and the forms had evidently been wrought with much care. It was rather the substance that eluded me. Was there, I wondered, any substance at all? It did not occur to me: suppose Enoch Soames was a fool! Up cropped a rival hypothesis: suppose *I* was! I inclined to give Soames the benefit of the doubt. I had read "*L'Après-midi d'un faune*" without extracting a glimmer of meaning; yet Mallarmé, of course, was a master. How was I to know that Soames wasn't another? There was a sort of music in his prose, not indeed arresting, but perhaps, I thought, haunting, and laden, perhaps, with meanings as deep as Mallarmé's own. I awaited his poems with an open mind.

And I looked forward to them with positive impatience after I had had a second meeting with him. This was on an evening in January. Going into the aforesaid domino-room, I had passed a table at which sat a pale man with an open book before him. He had looked from his book to me, and I looked back over my shoulder with a vague sense that I ought to have recognized him. I returned to pay my respects. After exchanging a few words, I said with a glance to the open book, "I see I am interrupting you," and was about to pass on, but, "I prefer," Soames replied in his toneless voice, "to be interrupted," and I obeyed his gesture that I should sit down.

I asked him if he often read here.

"Yes; things of this kind I read here," he answered, indicating the title of his book—"The Poems of Shelley."

"Anything that you really"—and I was going to say "admire?" But I cautiously left my sentence unfinished, and was glad that I had done so, for he said with unwonted emphasis, "Anything second-rate."

I had read little of Shelley, but, "Of course," I murmured, "he's very uneven."

"I should have thought evenness was just what was wrong with him. A deadly evenness. That's why I read him here. The noise of this place breaks the rhythm. He's tolerable here." Soames took up the book and glanced through the pages. He laughed. Soames's laugh was a short, single, and mirthless sound from the throat, unaccompanied by any movement of the face or brightening of the eyes. "What a period!" he uttered, laying the book down. And, "What a country!" he added.

I asked rather nervously if he didn't think Keats had more or less held his own against the drawbacks of time and place. He admitted that there were "passages in Keats," but did not specify them. Of "the older men," as he called them, he seemed to like only Milton. "Milton," he said, "wasn't sentimental." Also, "Milton had a dark insight." And again, "I can always read Milton in the reading-room."

"The reading-room?"

"Of the British Museum. I go there every day."

"You do? I've only been there once. I'm afraid I found it rather a depressing place. It—it seemed to sap one's vitality."

"It does. That's why I go there. The lower one's vitality, the more sensitive one is to great art. I live near the museum. I have rooms in Dyott Street."

"And you go round to the reading-room to read Milton?"

"Usually Milton." He looked at me. "It was Milton," he certificatively added, "who converted me to diabolism."

"Diabolism? Oh, yes? Really?" said I, with that vague discomfort and that intense desire to be polite which one feels when a man speaks of his own religion. "You—worship the devil?"

Soames shook his head.

"It's not exactly worship," he qualified, sipping his absinthe. "It's more a matter of trusting and encouraging."

"I see, yes. I had rather gathered from the preface to 'Negations' that you were a—a Catholic."

"*Je l'étais à cette époque.* In fact, I still am. I am a Catholic diabolist."

But this profession he made in an almost cursory tone. I could see that what was upmost in his mind was the fact that I had read "Negations." His pale eyes had for the first time gleamed. I felt as one who is about to be examined *viva voce* on the very subject in which he is shakiest. I hastily asked him how soon his poems were to be published.

"Next week," he told me.

"And are they to be published without a title?"

"No. I found a title at last. But I sha'n't tell you what it is," as though I had been so impertinent as to inquire. "I am not sure that it wholly satisfies me. But it is the best I can find. It suggests something of the quality of the poems—strange growths, natural and wild, yet exquisite," he added, "and many-hued, and full of poisons."

I asked him what he thought of Baudelaire. He uttered the snort that was his laugh, and, "Baudelaire," he said, "was a *bourgeois malgré lui*." France had had only one poet—Villon; "and two thirds of Villon were sheer journalism." Verlaine was "an *épicier malgré lui*." Altogether, rather to my surprise, he rated French literature lower than English. There were "passages" in *Villiers de l'Isle-Adam*. But, "I," he summed up, "owe nothing to France." He nodded at me. "You'll see," he predicted.

I did not, when the time came, quite see that. I thought the author of "Fungoids" did, unconsciously of course, owe something to the young Parisian decadents or to the young English ones who owed something to *them*. I still think so. The little book, bought by me in Oxford, lies before me as I write. Its pale-gray buckram cover and silver lettering have not worn well. Nor have its contents. Through these, with a melancholy interest, I have again been looking. They are not much. But at the time of their publication I had a vague suspicion that they *might* be. I suppose it is my capacity for faith, not poor Soames's work, that is weaker than it once was.

TO A YOUNG WOMAN

Thou art, who hast not been!
    Pale tunes irresolute
    And traceries of old sounds
    Blown from a rotted flute
Mingle with noise of cymbals rouged with rust,
Nor not strange forms and epicene
    Lie bleeding in the dust,
        Being wounded with wounds.
    For this it is
That in thy counterpart
    Of age-long mockeries
Thou hast not been nor art!

There seemed to me a certain inconsistency as between the first and last lines of this. I tried, with bent brows, to resolve the discord. But I did not take my failure as wholly incompatible with a meaning in Soames's mind. Might it not rather indicate the depth of his meaning? As for the craftsmanship, "rouged with rust" seemed to me a fine stroke, and "nor not" instead of "and" had a curious felicity. I wondered who the "young woman" was, and what she had made of it all. I sadly suspect that Soames could not have made more of it than she. Yet even now, if one doesn't try to make any sense at all of the poem, and reads it just for the sound, there is a certain grace of cadence. Soames was an artist, in so far as he was anything, poor fellow!

It seemed to me, when first I read "Fungoids," that, oddly enough, the diabolistic side of him was the best. Diabolism seemed to be a cheerful, even a wholesome, influence in his life.

NOCTURNE

Round and round the shutter'd Square
I strolled with the Devil's arm in mine.
No sound but the scrape of his hoofs was there
And the ring of his laughter and mine.
    We had drunk black wine.

I scream'd, "I will race you, Master!"
"What matter," he shriek'd, "to-night
Which of us runs the faster?

> *There is nothing to fear to-night*
>   *In the foul moon's light!"*
>
> Then I look'd him in the eyes
> And I laugh'd full shrill at the lie he told
> And the gnawing fear he would fain disguise.
> It was true, what I'd time and again been told:
>   He was old—old.

There was, I felt, quite a swing about that first stanza—a joyous and rollicking note of comradeship. The second was slightly hysterical, perhaps. But I liked the third, it was so bracingly unorthodox, even according to the tenets of Soames's peculiar sect in the faith. Not much "trusting and encouraging" here! Soames triumphantly exposing the devil as a liar, and laughing "full shrill," cut a quite heartening figure, I thought, then! Now, in the light of what befell, none of his other poems depresses me so much as "Nocturne."

I looked out for what the metropolitan reviewers would have to say. They seemed to fall into two classes: those who had little to say and those who had nothing. The second class was the larger, and the words of the first were cold; insomuch that

> Strikes a note of modernity. . . . These tripping numbers.—"The Preston Telegraph."

was the only lure offered in advertisements by Soames's publisher. I had hoped that when next I met the poet I could congratulate him on having made a stir, for I fancied he was not so sure of his intrinsic greatness as he seemed. I was but able to say, rather coarsely, when next I did see him, that I hoped "Fungoids" was "selling splendidly." He looked at me across his glass of absinthe and asked if I had bought a copy. His publisher had told him that three had been sold. I laughed, as at a jest.

"You don't suppose I *care*, do you?" he said, with something like a snarl. I disclaimed the notion. He added that he was not a tradesman. I said mildly that I wasn't, either, and murmured that an artist who gave truly new and great things to the world had always to wait long for recognition. He said he cared not a sou for recognition. I agreed that the act of creation was its own reward.

His moroseness might have alienated me if I had regarded myself as a nobody. But ah! hadn't both John Lane and Aubrey Beardsley suggested that I should write an essay for the great new venture that was afoot—"The Yellow Book"? And hadn't Henry Harland, as editor, accepted my essay? And wasn't it to be in the very first number? At Oxford I was still *in statu pupillari*. In London I regarded myself as very much indeed a graduate now—one whom no

Soames could ruffle. Partly to show off, partly in sheer good-will, I told Soames he ought to contribute to "The Yellow Book." He uttered from the throat a sound of scorn for that publication.

Nevertheless, I did, a day or two later, tentatively ask Harland if he knew anything of the work of a man called Enoch Soames. Harland paused in the midst of his characteristic stride around the room, threw up his hands toward the ceiling, and groaned aloud: he had often met "that absurd creature" in Paris, and this very morning had received some poems in manuscript from him.

"Has he *no* talent?" I asked.

"He has an income. He's all right." Harland was the most joyous of men and most generous of critics, and he hated to talk of anything about which he couldn't be enthusiastic. So I dropped the subject of Soames. The news that Soames had an income did take the edge off solicitude. I learned afterward that he was the son of an unsuccessful and deceased bookseller in Preston, but had inherited an annuity of three hundred pounds from a married aunt, and had no surviving relatives of any kind. Materially, then, he was "all right." But there was still a spiritual pathos about him, sharpened for me now by the possibility that even the praises of "The Preston Telegraph" might not have been forthcoming had he not been the son of a Preston man. He had a sort of weak doggedness which I could not but admire. Neither he nor his work received the slightest encouragement; but he persisted in behaving as a personage: always he kept his dingy little flag flying. Wherever congregated the *jeunes féroces* of the arts, in whatever Soho restaurant they had just discovered, in whatever music-hall they were most frequently, there was Soames in the midst of them, or, rather, on the fringe of them, a dim, but inevitable, figure. He never sought to propitiate his fellow-writers, never bated a jot of his arrogance about his own work or of his contempt for theirs. To the painters he was respectful, even humble; but for the poets and prosaists of "The Yellow Book" and later of "The Savoy" he had never a word but of scorn. He wasn't resented. It didn't occur to anybody that he or his Catholic diabolism mattered. When, in the autumn of '96, he brought out (at his own expense, this time) a third book, his last book, nobody said a word for or against it. I meant, but forgot, to buy it. I never saw it, and am ashamed to say I don't even remember what it was called. But I did, at the time of its publication, say to Rothenstein that I thought poor old Soames was really a rather tragic figure, and that I believed he would literally die for want of recognition. Rothenstein scoffed. He said I was trying to get credit for a kind heart which I didn't possess; and perhaps this was so. But at the private view of the New English Art Club, a few weeks later, I beheld a pastel portrait of "Enoch Soames, Esq." It was very like him, and very like Rothenstein to have done it. Soames was standing near it, in his soft hat and his waterproof cape, all through the afternoon. Anybody who knew him would have recognized the portrait at a glance, but nobody who didn't know him would have recognized the portrait from its bystander: it "existed" so much more than he; it was bound to. Also, it had not that expression of faint happiness which on that day was discernible, yes, in Soames's countenance. Fame had breathed on him. Twice again in the course of the month I went to the New English, and on both occasions Soames himself was on view there. Looking back, I regard the close of that exhibition as having been virtually the close of his career. He had felt the breath of Fame against his cheek—so late, for such a little while; and at its withdrawal he gave in, gave up, gave out. He, who had never looked strong or well, looked ghastly now—a shadow of the shade he had once been. He still frequented the domino-room, but having lost all wish to excite curiosity, he no longer read books there. "You read only at the museum now?" I asked, with attempted cheerfulness. He said he never went there now. "No absinthe there," he muttered. It was the sort of thing that in old days he would have said for effect; but it carried conviction now. Absinthe, erst but a point in the "personality" he had striven so hard to build up, was solace and necessity now. He no longer called it "*la sorcière glauque.*" He had shed away all his French phrases. He had become a plain, unvarnished Preston man.

Failure, if it be a plain, unvarnished, complete failure, and even though it be a squalid failure, has always a certain dignity. I avoided Soames because he made me feel rather vulgar. John Lane had published, by this time, two little books of mine, and they had had a pleasant little success of esteem. I was a—slight, but definite—"personality." Frank Harris had engaged me to kick up my heels in "The Saturday Review," Alfred Harmsworth was letting me do likewise in "The Daily Mail." I was just what Soames wasn't. And he shamed my gloss. Had I known that he really and firmly believed in the greatness of what he as an artist had achieved, I might not have shunned him. No man who hasn't lost his vanity can be held to have altogether failed. Soames's dignity was an illusion of mine. One day, in the first week of June, 1897, that illusion went. But on the evening of that day Soames went, too.

Enoch Soames

I had been out most of the morning and, as it was too late to reach home in time for luncheon, I sought the Vingtième. This little place—Restaurant du Vingtième Siècle, to give it its full title—had been discovered in '96 by the poets and prosaists, but had now been more or less abandoned in favor of some later find. I don't think it lived long enough to justify its name; but at that time there it still was, in Greek Street, a few doors from Soho Square, and almost opposite to that house where, in the first years of the century, a little girl, and with her a boy named De Quincey, made nightly encampment in darkness and hunger among dust and rats and old legal parchments. The Vingtième was but a small whitewashed room, leading out into the street at one end and into a kitchen at the other. The proprietor and cook was a Frenchman, known to us as Monsieur Vingtième; the waiters were his two daughters, Rose and Berthe; and the food, according to faith, was good. The tables were so narrow and were set so close together that there was space for twelve of them, six jutting from each wall.

Only the two nearest to the door, as I went in, were occupied. On one side sat a tall, flashy, rather Mephistophelian man whom I had seen from time to time in the domino-room and elsewhere. On the other side sat Soames. They made a queer contrast in that sunlit room, Soames sitting haggard in that hat and cape, which nowhere at any season had I seen him doff, and this other, this keenly vital man, at sight of whom I more than ever wondered whether he were a diamond merchant, a conjurer, or the head of a private detective agency. I was sure Soames didn't want my company; but I asked, as it would have seemed brutal not to, whether I might join him, and took the chair opposite to his. He was smoking a cigarette, with an untasted salmi of something on his plate and a half-empty bottle of Sauterne before him, and he was quite silent. I said that the preparations for the Jubilee made London impossible. (I rather liked them, really.) I professed a wish to go right away till the whole thing was over. In vain did I attune myself to his gloom. He seemed not to hear me or even to see me. I felt that his behavior made me ridiculous in the eyes of the other man. The gangway between the two rows of tables at the Vingtième was hardly more than two feet wide (Rose and Berthe, in their ministrations, had always to edge past each other, quarreling in whispers as they did so), and any one at the table abreast of yours was virtually at yours. I thought our neighbor was amused at my failure to interest Soames, and so, as I could not explain to him that my insistence was merely charitable, I became silent. Without turning my head, I had him well within my range of vision. I hoped I looked less vulgar than he in contrast with Soames. I was sure he was not an Englishman, but what *was* his nationality? Though his jet-black hair was *en brosse*, I did not think he was French. To Berthe, who waited on him, he spoke French fluently, but with a hardly native idiom and accent. I gathered that this was his first visit to the Vingtième; but Berthe was offhand in her manner to him: he had not made a good impression. His eyes were handsome, but, like the Vingtième's tables, too narrow and set too close together. His nose was predatory, and the points of his mustache, waxed up behind his nostrils, gave a fixity to his smile. Decidedly, he was sinister. And my sense of discomfort in his presence was intensified by the scarlet waistcoat which tightly, and so unseasonably in June, sheathed his ample chest. This waistcoat wasn't wrong merely because of the heat, either. It was somehow all wrong in itself. It wouldn't have done on Christmas morning. It would have struck a jarring note at the first night of "Hernani." I was trying to account for its wrongness when Soames suddenly and strangely broke silence. "A hundred years hence!" he murmured, as in a trance.

"We shall not be here," I briskly, but fatuously, added.

"We shall not be here. No," he droned, "but the museum will still be just where it is. And the reading-room just where it is. And people will be able to go and read there." He inhaled sharply, and a spasm as of actual pain contorted his features.

I wondered what train of thought poor Soames had been following. He did not enlighten me when he said, after a long pause, "You think I haven't minded."

"Minded what, Soames?"

"Neglect. Failure."

"*Failure?*" I said heartily. "Failure?" I repeated vaguely. "Neglect—yes, perhaps; but that's quite another matter. Of course you haven't been—appreciated. But what, then? Any artist who—who gives—" What I wanted to say was, "Any artist who gives truly new and great things to the world has always to wait long for recognition"; but the flattery would not out: in the face of his misery—a misery so genuine and so unmasked—my lips would not say the words.

And then he said them for me. I flushed. "That's what you were going to say, isn't it?" he asked.

"How did you know?"

"It's what you said to me three years ago, when 'Fungoids' was published." I flushed the more. I need not have flushed at all. "It's the only important thing I ever heard you say," he continued. "And I've never forgotten it. It's a true thing. It's a horrible truth. But d'you remember what I answered? I said, 'I don't care a sou for recognition.' And you believed me. You've gone on believing I'm above that sort of thing. You're shallow. What should *you* know of the feelings of a man like me? You imagine that a great artist's faith in himself and in the verdict of posterity is enough to keep him happy. You've never guessed at the bitterness and loneliness, the"—his voice broke; but presently he resumed, speaking with a force that I had never known in him. "Posterity! What use is it to *me?* A dead man doesn't know that people are visiting his grave, visiting his birthplace, putting up tablets to him, unveiling statues of him. A dead man can't read the books that are written about him. A hundred years hence! Think of it! If I could come back to life *then*—just for a few hours—and go to the reading-room and *read!* Or, better still, if I could be projected now, at this moment, into that future, into that reading-room, just for this one afternoon! I'd sell myself body and soul to the devil for that! Think of the pages and pages in the catalogue: 'Soames, Enoch' endlessly—endless editions, commentaries, prolegomena, biographies". But here he was interrupted by a sudden loud crack of the chair at the next table.

Our neighbor had half risen from his place. He was leaning toward us, apologetically intrusive.

"Excuse—permit me," he said softly. "I have been unable not to hear. Might I take a liberty? In this little restaurant-*sans-façon*—might I, as the phrase is, cut in?"

I could but signify our acquiescence. Berthe had appeared at the kitchen door, thinking the stranger wanted his bill. He waved her away with his cigar, and in another moment had seated himself beside me, commanding a full view of Soames.

"Though not an Englishman," he explained, "I know my London well, Mr. Soames. Your name and fame—Mr. Beerbohm's, too—very known to me. Your point is, who am *I?*" He glanced quickly over his shoulder, and in a lowered voice said, "I am the devil."

I couldn't help it; I laughed. I tried not to, I knew there was nothing to laugh at, my rudeness shamed me; but—I laughed with increasing volume. The devil's quiet dignity, the surprise and disgust of his raised eyebrows, did but the more dissolve me. I rocked to and fro; I lay back aching; I behaved deplorably.

"I am a gentleman, and," he said with intense emphasis, "I thought I was in the company of *gentlemen*."

"Don't!" I gasped faintly. "Oh, don't!"

"Curious, *nicht wahr*?" I heard him say to Soames. "There is a type of person to whom the very mention of my name is—oh, so awfully—funny! In your theaters the dullest *comédien* needs only to say 'The devil!' and right away they give him 'the loud laugh what speaks the vacant mind.' Is it not so?"

I had now just breath enough to offer my apologies. He accepted them, but coldly, and re-addressed himself to Soames.

"I am a man of business," he said, "and always I would put things through 'right now,' as they say in the States. You are a poet. *Les affaires*—you detest them. So be it. But with me you will deal, eh? What you have said just now gives me furiously to hope."

Soames had not moved except to light a fresh cigarette. He sat crouched forward, with his elbows squared on the table, and his head just above the level of his hands, staring up at the devil.

"Go on," he nodded. I had no remnant of laughter in me now.

"It will be the more pleasant, our little deal," the devil went on, "because you are—I mistake not?—a diabolist."

"A Catholic diabolist," said Soames.

The devil accepted the reservation genially.

"You wish," he resumed, "to visit now—this afternoon as-ever-is—the reading-room of the British Museum, yes? But of a hundred years hence, yes? *Parfaitement*. Time—an illusion. Past and future—they are as ever present as the present, or at any rate only what you call 'just round the corner.' I switch you on to any date. I project you—*pouf!* You wish to be in the reading-room just as it will be on the afternoon of June 3, 1997? You wish to find yourself standing in that room, just past the swing-doors, this very minute, yes? And to stay there till closing-time? Am I right?"

Soames nodded.

The devil looked at his watch. "Ten past two," he said. "Closing-time in summer same then as now—seven o'clock. That will give you almost five hours. At seven o'clock—*pouf!*—you find yourself again here, sitting at this table. I am dining to-night *dans le monde—dans le higlif*. That concludes my present visit to your great city. I come and fetch you here, Mr. Soames, on my way home."

"Home?" I echoed.

"Be it never so humble!" said the devil, lightly.

"All right," said Soames.

"Soames!" I entreated. But my friend moved not a muscle.

The devil had made as though to stretch forth

his hand across the table, but he paused in his gesture.

"A hundred years hence, as now," he smiled, "no smoking allowed in the reading-room. You would better therefore—"

Soames removed the cigarette from his mouth and dropped it into his glass of Sauterne.

"Soames!" again I cried. "Can't you"—but the devil had now stretched forth his hand across the table. He brought it slowly down on the table-cloth. Soames's chair was empty. His cigarette floated sodden in his wine-glass. There was no other trace of him.

For a few moments the devil let his hand rest where it lay, gazing at me out of the corners of his eyes, vulgarly triumphant.

A shudder shook me. With an effort I controlled myself and rose from my chair. "Very clever," I said condescendingly. "But—'The Time Machine' is a delightful book, don't you think? So entirely original!"

"You are pleased to sneer," said the devil, who had also risen, "but it is one thing to write about an impossible machine; it is a quite other thing to be a supernatural power." All the same, I had scored.

Berthe had come forth at the sound of our rising. I explained to her that Mr. Soames had been called away, and that both he and I would be dining here. It was not until I was out in the open air that I began to feel giddy. I have but the haziest recollection of what I did, where I wandered, in the glaring sunshine of that endless afternoon. I remember the sound of carpenters' hammers all along Piccadilly and the bare chaotic look of the half-erected "stands." Was it in the Green Park or in Kensington Gardens or *where* was it that I sat on a chair beneath a tree, trying to read an evening paper? There was a phrase in the leading article that went on repeating itself in my fagged mind: "Little is hidden from this august Lady full of the garnered wisdom of sixty years of Sovereignty." I remember wildly conceiving a letter (to reach Windsor by an express messenger told to await answer): "Madam: Well knowing that your Majesty is full of the garnered wisdom of sixty years of Sovereignty, I venture to ask your advice in the following delicate matter. Mr. Enoch Soames, whose poems you may or may not know—" Was there *no* way of helping him, saving him? A bargain was a bargain, and I was the last man to aid or abet any one in wriggling out of a reasonable obligation. I wouldn't have lifted a little finger to save *Faust*. But poor Soames! Doomed to pay without respite an eternal price for nothing but a fruitless search and a bitter disillusioning.

Odd and uncanny it seemed to me that he, Soames, in the flesh, in the waterproof cape, was at this moment living in the last decade of the next century, poring over books not yet written, and seeing and seen by men not yet born. Uncannier and odder still that to-night and evermore he would be in hell. Assuredly, truth was stranger than fiction.

Endless that afternoon was. Almost I wished I had gone with Soames, not, indeed, to stay in the reading-room, but to sally forth for a brisk sight-seeing walk around a new London. I wandered restlessly out of the park I had sat in. Vainly I tried to imagine myself an ardent tourist from the eighteenth century. Intolerable was the strain of the slow-passing and empty minutes. Long before seven o'clock I was back at the Vingtième.

I sat there just where I had sat for luncheon. Air came in listlessly through the open door behind me. Now and again Rose or Berthe appeared for a moment. I had told them I would not order any dinner till Mr. Soames came. A hurdy-gurdy began to play, abruptly drowning the noise of a quarrel between some Frenchmen farther up the street. Whenever the tune was changed I heard the quarrel still raging. I had bought another evening paper on my way. I unfolded it. My eyes gazed ever away from it to the clock over the kitchen door.

Five minutes now to the hour! I remembered that clocks in restaurants are kept five minutes fast. I concentrated my eyes on the paper. I vowed I would not look away from it again. I held it upright, at its full width, close to my face, so that I had no view of anything but it. Rather a tremulous sheet? Only because of the draft, I told myself.

My arms gradually became stiff; they ached; but I could not drop them—now. I had a suspicion, I had a certainty. Well, what, then? What else had I come for? Yet I held tight that barrier of newspaper. Only the sound of Berthe's brisk footstep from the kitchen enabled me, forced me, to drop it, and to utter:

"What shall we have to eat, Soames?"

"*Il est souffrant, ce pauvre Monsieur Soames?*" asked Berthe.

"He's only—tired." I asked her to get some wine—Burgundy—and whatever food might be ready. Soames sat crouched forward against the table exactly as when last I had seen him. It was as though he had never moved—he who had moved so unimaginably far. Once or twice in the afternoon it had for an instant occurred to me that perhaps his journey was not to be fruitless, that perhaps we had all been wrong in our estimate of the works of Enoch Soames. That we had been horribly right was horribly clear from the look of him. But, "Don't be discouraged," I falteringly said. "Perhaps it's only that you—didn't leave enough time. Two, three centuries hence, perhaps—"

"Yes," his voice came; "I've thought of that."

"And now—now for the more immediate future! Where are you going to hide? How would it be if you caught the Paris express from Charing Cross? Almost an hour to spare. Don't go on to Paris. Stop at Calais. Live in Calais. He'd never think of looking for you in Calais."

"It's like my luck," he said, "to spend my last hours on earth with an ass." But I was not offended. "And a treacherous ass," he strangely added, tossing across to me a crumpled bit of paper which he had been holding in his hand. I glanced at the writing on it—some sort of gibberish, apparently. I laid it impatiently aside.

"Come, Soames, pull yourself together! This isn't a mere matter of life or death. It's a question of eternal torment, mind you! You don't mean to say you're going to wait limply here till the devil comes to fetch you."

"I can't do anything else. I've no choice."

"Come! This is 'trusting and encouraging' with a

vengeance! This is diabolism run mad!" I filled his glass with wine. "Surely, now that you've *seen* the brute—"

"It's no good abusing him."

"You must admit there's nothing Miltonic about him, Soames."

"I don't say he's not rather different from what I expected."

"He's a vulgarian, he's a swell mobsman, he's the sort of man who hangs about the corridors of trains going to the Riviera and steals ladies' jewel-cases. Imagine eternal torment presided over by *him!*"

"You don't suppose I look forward to it, do you?"

"Then why not slip quietly out of the way?"

Again and again I filled his glass, and always, mechanically, he emptied it; but the wine kindled no spark of enterprise in him. He did not eat, and I myself ate hardly at all. I did not in my heart believe that any dash for freedom could save him. The chase would be swift, the capture certain. But better anything than this passive, meek, miserable waiting. I told Soames that for the honor of the human race he ought to make some show of resistance. He asked what the human race had ever done for him. "Besides," he said, "can't you understand that I'm in his power? You saw him touch me, didn't you? There's an end of it. I've no will. I'm sealed."

I made a gesture of despair. He went on repeating the word "sealed." I began to realize that the wine had clouded his brain. No wonder! Foodless he had gone into futurity, foodless he still was. I urged him to eat, at any rate, some bread. It was maddening to think that he, who had so much to tell, might tell nothing. "How was it all," I asked, "yonder? Come, tell me your adventures!"

"They'd make first-rate 'copy,' wouldn't they?"

"I'm awfully sorry for you, Soames, and I make all possible allowances; but what earthly right have you to insinuate that I should make 'copy,' as you call it, out of you?"

The poor fellow pressed his hands to his forehead.

"I don't know," he said. "I had some reason, I know. I'll try to remember." He sat plunged in thought.

"That's right. Try to remember everything. Eat a little more bread. What did the reading-room look like?"

"Much as usual," he at length muttered.

"Many people there?"

"Usual sort of number."

"What did they look like?"

Soames tried to visualize them.

"They all," he presently remembered, "looked very like one another."

My mind took a fearsome leap.

"All dressed in sanitary woolen?"

"Yes, I think so. Grayish-yellowish stuff."

"A sort of uniform?" He nodded. "With a number on it perhaps—a number on a large disk of metal strapped round the left arm? D. K. F. 78,910—that sort of thing?" It was even so. "And all of them, men and women alike, looking very well cared for? Very Utopian, and smelling rather strongly of carbolic, and all of them quite hairless?" I was right every time. Soames was only not sure whether the men and women were hairless or shorn. "I hadn't time to look at them very closely," he explained.

"No, of course not. But—"

"They stared at *me*, I can tell you. I attracted a great deal of attention." At last he had done that! "I think I rather scared them. They moved away whenever I came near. They followed me about, at a distance, wherever I went. The men at the round desk in the middle seemed to have a sort of panic whenever I went to make inquiries."

"What did you do when you arrived?"

Well, he had gone straight to the catalogue, of

course,—to the S volumes,—and had stood long before SN-SOF, unable to take this volume out of the shelf because his heart was beating so. At first, he said, he wasn't disappointed; he only thought there was some new arrangement. He went to the middle desk and asked where the catalogue of *twentieth-century* books was kept. He gathered that there was still only one catalogue. Again he looked up his name, stared at the three little pasted slips he had known so well. Then he went and sat down for a long time.

"And then," he droned, "I looked up the 'Dictionary of National Biography,' and some encyclopedias. I went back to the middle desk and asked what was the best modern book on late nineteenth-century literature. They told me Mr. T. K. Nupton's book was considered the best. I looked it up in the catalogue and filled in a form for it. It was brought to me. My name wasn't in the index, but yes!" he said with a sudden change of tone, "that's what I'd forgotten. Where's that bit of paper? Give it me back."

I, too, had forgotten that cryptic screed. I found it fallen on the floor, and handed it to him.

He smoothed it out, nodding and smiling at me disagreeably.

"I found myself glancing through Nupton's

book," he resumed. "Not very easy reading. Some sort of phonetic spelling. All the modern books I saw were phonetic."

"Then I don't want to hear any more, Soames, please."

"The proper names seemed all to be spelt in the old way. But for that I mightn't have noticed my own name."

"Your own name? Really? Soames, I'm *very* glad."

"And yours."

"No!"

"I thought I should find you waiting here to-night, so I took the trouble to copy out the passage. Read it."

I snatched the paper. Soames's handwriting was characteristically dim. It and the noisome spelling and my excitement made me all the slower to grasp what T. K. Nupton was driving at.

The document lies before me at this moment. Strange that the words I here copy out for you were copied out for me by poor Soames just eighty-two years hence!

From page 234 of "Inglish Littracher 1890–1900" bi T. K. Nupton, publishd bi th Stait, 1992.

Enoch Soames

Fr egzarmpl, a riter ov th time, naimed Max Beerbohm, hoo woz stil alive in th twentith senchri, rote a stauri in wich e pautraid an immajnari karrakter kauld "Enoch Soames"— a thurd-rait poit boo heleevz imself a grate jeneus an maix a bargin with th Devvl in auder ter no wot posterriti thinx ov im! It iz a sumwot labud sattire, but not without vallu az showing hon seriusli the yung men ov th aiteen-ninetiz took themselvz. Nou that th littreri profeshn haz bin auganized az a departmnt of publik servis, our riters hav found their levvl an hav lernt ter doo their duti without thort ov th morro. "Th laibrer iz werthi ov hiz hire" an that iz aul. Thank hevvn we hav no Enoch Soameses amung us to-dai!

I found that by murmuring the words aloud (a device which I commend to my reader) I was able to master them little by little. The clearer they became, the greater was my bewilderment, my distress and horror. The whole thing was a nightmare. Afar, the great grisly background of what was in store for the poor dear art of letters; here, at the table, fixing on me a gaze that made me hot all over, the poor fellow whom—whom evidently—but no:

whatever down-grade my character might take in coming years, I should never be such a brute as to—

Again I examined the screed. "Immajnari." But here Soames was, no more imaginary, alas! than I. And "labud"—what on earth was that? (To this day I have never made out that word.) "It's all very—baffling," I at length stammered.

Soames said nothing, but cruelly did not cease to look at me.

"Are you sure," I temporized, "quite sure you copied the thing out correctly?"

"Quite."

"Well, then, it's this wretched Nupton who must have made—must be going to make—some idiotic mistake. Look here, Soames, you know me better than to suppose that I—After all, the name Max Beerbohm is not at all an uncommon one, and there must be several Enoch Soameses running around, or, rather, Enoch Soames is a name that might occur to any one writing a story. And I don't write stories; I'm an essayist, an observer, a recorder. I admit that it's an extraordinary coincidence. But you must see—"

"I see the whole thing," said Soames, quietly. And he added, with a touch of his old manner, but with more dignity than I had ever known in him, "*Parlons d'autre chose.*"

I accepted that suggestion very promptly. I returned straight to the more immediate future. I spent most of the long evening in renewed appeals to Soames to come away and seek refuge somewhere. I remember saying at last that if indeed I was destined to write about him, the supposed "stauri" had better have at least a happy ending. Soames repeated those last three words in a tone of intense scorn.

"In life and in art," he said, "all that matters is an *inevitable* ending."

"But," I urged more hopefully than I felt, "an ending that can be avoided *isn't* inevitable."

"You aren't an artist," he rasped. "And you're so hopelessly not an artist that, so far from being able to imagine a thing and make it seem true, you're going to make even a true thing seem as if you'd made it up. You're a miserable bungler. And it's like my luck."

I protested that the miserable bungler was not I, was not going to be I, but T. K. Nupton; and we had a rather heated argument, in the thick of which it suddenly seemed to me that Soames saw he was in the wrong: he had quite physically cowered. But I wondered why—and now I guessed with a cold throb just why—he stared so past me. The bringer of that "inevitable ending" filled the doorway.

I managed to turn in my chair and to say, not without a semblance of lightness, "Aha, come in!" Dread was indeed rather blunted in me by his looking so absurdly like a villain in a melodrama. The sheen of his tilted hat and of his shirt-front, the repeated twists he was giving to his mustache, and most of all the magnificence of his sneer, gave token that he was there only to be foiled.

He was at our table in a stride. "I am sorry," he sneered witheringly, "to break up your pleasant party, but—"

"You don't; you complete it," I assured him. "Mr. Soames and I want to have a little talk with you. Won't you sit? Mr. Soames got nothing, frankly nothing, by his journey this afternoon. We don't wish to say that the whole thing was a swindle, a common swindle. On the contrary, we believe you meant well. But of course the bargain, such as it was, is off."

The devil gave no verbal answer. He merely looked at Soames and pointed with rigid forefinger to the door. Soames was wretchedly rising from his chair when, with a desperate, quick gesture, I swept together two dinner-knives that were on the table, and laid their blades across each other. The devil stepped sharp back against the table behind him, averting his face and shuddering.

"You are not superstitious!" he hissed.

"Not at all," I smiled.

"Soames," he said as to an underling, but without turning his face, "put those knives straight!"

With an inhibitive gesture to my friend, "Mr. Soames," I said emphatically to the devil, "is a *Catholic* diabolist"; but my poor friend did the devil's bidding, not mine; and now, with his master's eyes again fixed on him, he arose, he shuffled past me. I tried to speak. It was he that spoke. "Try," was the prayer he threw back at me as the devil pushed him roughly out through the door—"*try* to make them know that I did exist!"

In another instant I, too, was through that door. I stood staring all ways, up the street, across it, down it. There was moonlight and lamplight, but there was not Soames nor that other.

Dazed, I stood there. Dazed, I turned back at length into the little room, and I suppose I paid Berthe or Rose for my dinner and luncheon and for Soames's; I hope so, for I never went to the Vingtième again. Ever since that night I have avoided Greek Street altogether. And for years I did not set foot even in Soho Square, because on that same night it was there that I paced and loitered, long and long, with some such dull sense of hope as a man has in not straying far from the place where he has lost something. "Round and round the shutter'd Square"—that line came back to me on my lonely beat, and with it the whole stanza, ringing in my brain and bearing in on me how tragically different from the happy scene imagined by him was the poet's actual experience of that prince in whom of all princes we should put not our trust!

But strange how the mind of an essayist, be it never so stricken, roves and ranges! I remember pausing before a wide door-step and wondering if perchance it was on this very one that the young De Quincey lay ill and faint while poor Ann flew as fast as her feet would carry her to Oxford Street, the "stony-hearted stepmother" of them both, and came back bearing that "glass of port wine and spices" but for which he might, so he thought, actually have died. Was this the very door-step that the old De Quincey used to revisit in homage? I pondered Ann's fate, the cause of her sudden vanishing from the ken of her boy friend; and presently I blamed myself for letting the past override the present. Poor vanished Soames!

And for myself, too, I began to be troubled. What had I better do? Would there be a hue and cry—"Mysterious Disappearance of an Author," and all that? He had last been seen lunching and dining in my company. Hadn't I better get a hansom and drive straight to Scotland Yard? They would think I was a lunatic. After all, I reassured myself, London was a very large place, and one very dim figure might easily drop out of it unobserved, now especially, in the blinding glare of the near Jubilee. Better say nothing at all, I thought.

And I was right. Soames's disappearance made no stir at all. He was utterly forgotten before any one, so far as I am aware, noticed that he was no longer hanging around. Now and again some poet or prosaist may have said to another, "What has become of that man Soames?" but I never heard any such question asked. As for his landlady in Dyott Street, no doubt he had paid her weekly, and what possessions he may have had in his rooms were enough to save her from fretting. The solicitor through whom he was paid his annuity may be presumed to have made inquiries, but no echo of these resounded. There was something rather ghastly to me in the general unconsciousness that Soames had existed, and more than once I caught myself wondering whether Nupton, that babe unborn, were going to be right in thinking him a figment of my brain.

In that extract from Nupton's repulsive book there is one point which perhaps puzzles you. How is it that the author, though I have here mentioned him by name and have quoted the exact words he is going to write, is not going to grasp the obvious corollary that I have invented nothing? The answer can be only this: Nupton will not have read the later passages of this memoir. Such lack of thoroughness is a serious fault in any one who undertakes to do scholar's work. And I hope these words will meet the eye of some contemporary rival to Nupton and be the undoing of Nupton.

I like to think that some time between 1992 and 1997 somebody will have looked up this memoir, and will have forced on the world his inevitable and startling conclusions. And I have reason for believing that this will be so. You realize that the reading-room into which Soames was projected by the devil was in all respects precisely as it will be on the afternoon of June 3, 1997. You realize, therefore, that on that afternoon, when it comes round, there the selfsame crowd will be, and there Soames will be, punctually, he and they doing precisely what they did before. Recall now Soames's account of the sensation he made. You may say that the mere difference of his costume was enough to make him sensational in that uniformed crowd. You wouldn't say so if you had ever seen him, and I assure you that in no period would Soames be anything but dim. The fact that people are going to stare at him and follow him around and seem afraid of him, can be explained only on the hypothesis that they will somehow have been prepared for his ghostly visitation. They will have been awfully waiting to see whether he really would come. And when he does come the effect will of course be—awful.

An authentic, guaranteed, proved ghost, but only a ghost, alas! Only that. In his first visit Soames was a creature of flesh and blood, whereas the creatures among whom he was projected were but ghosts, I take it—solid, palpable, vocal, but unconscious and automatic ghosts, in a building that was itself an illusion. Next time that building and those creatures will be real. It is of Soames that there will be but the semblance. I wish I could think him destined to revisit the world actually, physically, consciously. I wish he had this one brief escape, this one small treat, to look forward to. I never forget him for long. He is where he is and forever. The more rigid moralists among you may say he has only himself to blame. For my part, I think he has been very hardly used. It is well that vanity should be chastened; and Enoch Soames's vanity was, I admit, above the average, and called for special treatment. But there was no need for vindictiveness. You say he contracted to pay the price he is paying. Yes; but I maintain that he was induced to do so by fraud. Well informed in all things, the devil must have known that my friend would gain nothing by his visit to futurity. The whole thing was a very shabby trick. The more I think of it, the more detestable the devil seems to me.

Of him I have caught sight several times, here and there, since that day at the Vingtième. Only once, however, have I seen him at close quarters. This was a couple of years ago, in Paris. I was walking one afternoon along the rue d'Antin, and I saw him advancing from the opposite direction, over-dressed as ever, and swinging an ebony cane and altogether behaving as though the whole pavement belonged to him. At thought of Enoch Soames and the myriads of other sufferers eternally in this brute's dominion, a great cold wrath filled me, and I drew myself up to my full height. But—well, one is so used to nodding and smiling in the street to anybody whom one knows that the action becomes almost independent of oneself; to prevent it requires a very sharp effort and great presence of mind. I was miserably aware, as I passed the devil, that I nodded and smiled to him. And my shame was the deeper and hotter because he, if you please, stared straight at me with the utmost haughtiness.

To be cut, deliberately cut, by *him!* I was, I still am, furious at having had that happen to me.

RICHARD BRUCE NUGENT

Smoke, Lilies and Jade

He wanted to do something . . . to write or draw . . . or something . . . but it was so comfortable just to lay there on the bed . . . his shoes off . . . and think . . . think of everything . . . short disconnected thoughts—to wonder . . . to remember . . . to think and smoke . . . why wasn't he worried that he had no money . . . he *had* had five cents . . . but he had been hungry . . . he *was* hungry and still . . . all he wanted to do was . . . lay there comfortably smoking . . . think . . . wishing he were writing . . . or drawing . . . or something . . . something about the things he felt and thought . . . but what did he think . . . he remembered how his mother had awakened him one night . . . ages ago . . . six years ago . . . Alex . . . he had always wondered at the strangeness of it . . . she had seemed so . . . so . . . so just the same . . . Alex . . . I think your father is dead . . . and it hadn't seemed so strange . . . yet . . . one's mother didn't say that . . . didn't wake one at midnight every night to say . . . feel him . . . put your hand on his head . . . then whisper with a catch in her voice . . . I'm afraid . . . sh don't wake Lam . . . yet it hadn't seemed as it should have seemed . . . even when he had felt his father's cool wet forehead . . . it hadn't been tragic . . . the light had been turned very low . . . and flickered . . . yet it hadn't been tragic . . . or weird . . . not at all as one should feel when one's father died . . . even his reply of . . . yes he is dead . . . had been commonplace . . . hadn't been dramatic . . . there had been no tears . . . no sobs . . . not even a sorrow . . . and yet he must have realized that one's father couldn't smile . . . or sing any more . . . after he had died . . . every one remembered his father's voice . . . it had been a lush voice . . . a promise . . . then that dressing together . . . his mother and himself . . . in the bathroom . . . why was the bathroom always the warmest room in the winter . . . as they had put on their clothes . . . his mother had been telling him what he must do . . . and cried softly . . . and that had made him cry too but you mustn't cry Alex . . . remember you have to be a little man now . . . and that was all . . . didn't other wives and sons cry more for their dead than that . . . anyway people never cried for beautiful sunsets . . . or music . . . and those were the things that hurt . . . the things to sympathize with . . . then out into the snow and dark of the morning . . . first to the undertaker's . . . no first to Uncle Frank's . . . why did Aunt Lula have to act like that . . . to ask again and again . . . but when did he die . . . when did he die . . . I just can't believe it . . . poor Minerva . . . then out into the snow and dark again . . . how had his mother expected him to know where to find the night bell at the undertaker's . . . he was the most sensible of them all tho . . . all he had said was . . . what . . . Harry Francis . . . too bad . . . tell mamma I'll be there first thing in the morning . . . then down the deserted streets again . . . to grandmother's . . . it was growing light now . . . it must be terrible to die in daylight . . . grandpa had been sweeping the snow off the yard . . . he had been glad of that because . . . well he could tell him better than grandma . . . grandpa . . . father's dead . . . and he hadn't acted strange either . . . books lied . . . he had just looked at Alex a moment then continued sweeping . . . all he said was . . . what time did he die . . . she'll want to know . . . then passing thru the lonesome street toward home . . . Mrs. Mamie Grant was closing a window and spied him . . . hallow Alex . . . an' how's your father this mornin' . . . dead . . . get out . . . tch tch tch an' I was just around there with a cup a' custard yesterday . . . Alex puffed contentedly on his cigarette . . . he was hungry and comfortable . . . and he had an ivory holder inlaid with red jade and green . . . funny how the smoke seemed to climb up that ray of sunlight . . . went up the slant just like imagination . . . was imagination blue . . . or was it because he had spent his last five cents and couldn't worry . . . anyway it was nice to lay there and wonder . . . and remember . . . why was he so different from other people . . . the only things he remebered of his father's funeral were the crowded church and the ride in the hack . . . so many people there in the church . . . and ladies with tears in their eyes . . . and on their cheeks . . . and some men too . . . why did people cry . . . vanity that was all . . . yet they weren't exactly hypocrites . . . but why . . . it had made him furious . . . all these people crying . . . it wasn't *their* father . . . and he wasn't crying . . . couldn't cry for sorrow altho he had loved his father more than . . . than . . . it had made him so angry that tears had come to his eyes . . . and he had been ashamed of his mother . . . crying into a handkerchief . . . so ashamed that tears had run down his cheeks and he had frowned . . . and some one . . . a woman . . . had said . . . look at that poor little dear . . . Alex is just like his father . . . and the tears had run fast . . . because he *wasn't* like his father . . . he couldn't sing . . . he didn't want to sing . . . he didn't want to sing . . . Alex blew a cloud of smoke . . . blue smoke . . . when they had taken his father from the vault three weeks later . . . he had grown beautiful . . . his nose had become perfect and clear . . . his hair had turned jet black and glossy and silky . . . and his skin was a transparent green . . . like the sea only not so deep . . . and where it was drawn over the cheek bones a pale beautiful red appeared . . . like a blush . . . why hadn't his father looked like that always . . . but no . . . to have sung would have broken the wondrous repose of his lips and maybe that was his beauty . . . maybe it was wrong to think thoughts like these . . . but they were nice and pleasant and comfortable . . . when one was smoking a cigarette thru an ivory holder . . . inlaid with red jade and green . . . .

he wondered why he couldn't find work . . . a job . . . when he had first come to New York he had . . . and he had only been fourteen then was it because he was nineteen now that he felt so idle . . . and contented . . . or because he was an artist . . . but was he an artist . . . was one an artist until one became known . . . of course he was an artist . . . and strangely enough so were all his friends . . . he should be ashamed that he didn't work . . . but . . . was it five years in New York . . . or the fact that he was an artist . . . when his mother said she couldn't understand him . . . why did he vaguely pity her instead of being ashamed . . . he should be . . . his mother and all his relatives said so . . . his brother was three years younger than he and yet he had already been away from home a year . . . on the stage . . . making thirty-five dollars a week . . . had three suits and many clothes and was going to help mother . . . while he . . . Alex . . . was content to lay and smoke and meet friends at night . . . to argue and read Wilde . . . Freud . . . Boccaccio and Schnitzler . . . to attend Gurdjieff meetings and know things . . . Why did they scoff at him for knowing such people as Carl . . . Mencken . . . Toomer . . . Hughes . . . Cullen . . . Wood . . . Cabell . . . oh the whole lot of them . . . was it because it seemed incongruous that he . . . who was so little known . . . should call by first names people they would like to know . . . were they jealous . . . no mothers aren't jealous of their sons . . . they are proud of them . . . why then . . . when these friends accepted and liked him . . . no matter how he dressed . . . why did mother ask . . . and you went looking like that . . . Langston was a fine fellow . . . he knew there was something in Alex . . . and so did Rene and Borgia . . . and Zora and Clement and Miguel . . . and . . . and . . . and all of them . . . if he went to see mother she would ask . . . how do you feel Alex with nothing in your pockets . . . I don't see how you can be satisfied . . . Really you're a mystery to me . . . and who you take after . . . I'm sure I don't know . . . none of my brothers were lazy and shiftless . . . I can never remember the time when they weren't sending money home and your father was your age he was supporting a family . . . where you get your nerve I don't know . . . just because you've tried to write one or two little poems and stories that no one understands . . . you seem to think the world owes you a living . . . you should see by now how much is thought of them . . . you can't sell anything . . . and you won't do anything to make money . . . wake up Alex . . . I don't know what will become of you . . . .

it was hard to believe in one's self after that . . . did Wilde's parents or Shelley's or Goya's talk to them like that . . . but it was depressing to think in that vein . . . Alex stretched and yawned . . . Max had died . . . Margaret had died . . . so had Sonia . . . Cynthia . . . Juan-Jose and Harry . . . all people he had loved . . . loved one by one and together . . . and all had died . . . he never loved a person long before they died . . . in truth he was tragic . . . that was a lovely appellation . . . The Tragic Genius . . . think . . . to go thru life known as The Tragic Genius . . . romantic . . . but it was more or less true . . . Alex turned over and blew another cloud of smoke . . . was all life like that . . . smoke . . . blue smoke from an ivory holder . . . he wished he were in New Bedford . . . New Bedford was a nice place . . . snug little houses set complacently behind protecting lawns . . . half open windows showing prim interiors from behind waving cool curtains . . . inviting . . . like precise courtesans winking from behind lace fans . . . and trees . . . many trees . . . casting lacey patterns of shade on the sun dipped sidewalks . . . small stores . . . naively proud of their pseudo grandeur . . . banks . . . called institutions for saving . . . all naive . . . that was it . . . New Bedford was naive . . . after the sophistication of New York it would fan one like a refreshing breeze . . . and yet he had returned to New York . . . and sophistication . . . was he sophisticated . . . no because he was seldom bored . . . seldom bored by anything . . . and weren't the sophisticated continually suffering from ennui . . . on the contrary . . . he was amused . . . amused by the artificiality of naivety and sophistication alike . . . but may be that in itself was the essence of sophistication or . . . was it cynicism . . . or were the two identical . . . he blew a cloud of smoke . . . it was growing dark now . . . and the smoke no longer had a ladder to climb . . . but soon the moon would rise and then he would clothe the silver moon in blue smoke garments . . . truly smoke was like imagination . . . .

Alex sat up . . . pulled on his shoes and went out . . . it was a beautiful night . . . and so large . . . the dusky blue hung like a curtain in an immense arched doorway . . . fastened with silver tacks . . . to wander in the night was wonderful . . . myriads of inquisitive lights . . . curiously prying into the dark . . . and fading unsatisfied . . . he passed a woman . . . she was not beautiful . . . and he was sad because she did not weep that she would never be beautiful . . . was it Wilde who had said . . . a cigarette is the most perfect pleasure because it leaves one unsatisfied . . . the breeze gave to him a perfume stolen from some wandering lady of the evening . . . it pleased him . . . why was it that men wouldn't use perfumes . . . they should . . . each and every one of them liked perfumes . . . the man who denied that was a liar . . . or a coward . . . but if ever he were to voice that though . . . express it . . . he would be misunderstood . . . a fine feeling that . . . to be misunderstood . . . it made him feel tragic and great . . . but may be it would be nicer to be understood . . . but no . . . no great artist is . . . then again neither were fools . . . they were strangely akin these two . . . Alex thought of a sketch he would make . . . a personality sketch of Fania . . . straight classic features tinted proud purple . . . sensuous fine lips . . . gilded for truth . . . eyes . . . half opened and lids colored mysterious green . . . hair black and straight . . . drawn sternly mocking back from the false puritanical forehead . . . maybe he would make Edith too . . . skin a blue . . . infinite like night . . . and eyes . . . slant and grey . . . very complacent like a cat's . . . Mona Lisa lips . . . red and seductive as . . . as pomegranate juice . . . in truth it was fine to be young and hungry and an artist . . . to blow blue smoke from an ivory holder . . . .

here was the cafeteria . . . it was almost as tho it had journeyed to meet him . . . the night was so blue . . . how does blue feel . . . or red or gold or any other color . . . if colors could be heard he could paint most wondrous tunes . . . symphonious . . . think . . . the dulcet clear tone of a blue like night . . . of a red like pomegranate juice . . . like Edith's lips . . . of the fairy tones to be heard in a sunset . . . like rubies shaken in a crystal cup . . . of the symphony of Fania . . . and silver . . . and gold . . . he had heard the sound of gold . . . but they weren't the sounds he wanted to catch . . . no . . . they must be liquid . . . not so staccato but flowing variations of the same caliber . . . there was no one in the cafe as yet . . . he sat and waited . . . that was a clever idea he had had about color music . . . but

Smoke, Lilies and Jade

after all he was a monstrous clever fellow . . . Jurgen had said that . . . funny how characters in books said the things one wanted to say . . . he would like to know Jurgen . . . how does one go about getting an introduction to a fiction character . . . go up to the brown cover of the book and knock gently . . . and say hello . . . then timidly . . . is Duke Jurgen there . . . or . . . no because if entered the book in the beginning Jurgen would only be a pawn broker . . . and one didn't enter a book in the center . . . but what foolishness . . . Alex lit a cigarette . . . but Cabell was a master to have written Jurgen . . . and an artist . . . and a poet . . . Alex blew a cloud of smoke . . . a few lines of one of Langston's poems came to describe Jurgen . . . . .

> Somewhat like Ariel
> Somewhat like Puck
> Somewhat like a gutter boy
> Who loves to play in muck.
> Somewhat like Bacchus
> Somewhat like Pan
> And a way with women
> Like a sailor man . . . .

Langston must have known Jurgen . . . suppose Jurgen had met Tonio Kroeger . . . what a vagrant thought . . . Kroeger . . . Kroeger . . . Kroeger . . .

why here was Rene . . . Alex had almost gone to sleep . . . Alex blew a cone of smoke as he took Rene's hand . . . it was nice to have friends like Rene . . . so comfortable . . . Rene was speaking . . . Borgia joined them . . . and de Diego Padro . . . their talk veered to . . . James Branch Cabell . . . beautiful . . . marvelous . . . Rene had an enchanting accent . . . said sank for thank and souse for south . . . but they couldn't know Cabell's greatness . . . Alex searched the smoke for expression . . . he . . . he . . . well he has created a phantasy mire . . . that's it . . . from clear rich imagery . . . life and silver sands . . . that's nice . . . and silver sands . . . imagine lilies growing in such a mire . . . when they close at night their gilded underside would protect . . . but that's not it at all . . . his thoughts just carried and mingled like . . . like odors . . . suggested but never definite . . . Rene was leaving . . . they all were leaving . . . Alex sauntered slowly back . . . the houses all looked sleepy . . . funny . . . made him feel like writing poetry . . . and about death too . . . an elevator crashed by overhead scattering all his thoughts with its noise . . . making them spread . . . in circles . . . then larger circles . . . just like a splash in a calm pool . . . what had he been thinking . . . of . . . a poem about death . . . but he no longer felt that urge . . . just walk and

Smoke, Lilies and Jade

think and wonder . . . think and remember and smoke . . . blow smoke that mixed with his thoughts and the night . . . he would like to live in a large white palace . . . to wear a long black cape . . . very full and lined with vermillion . . . to have many cushions and to lie there among them . . . talking to his friends . . . lie there in a yellow silk shirt and black velvet trousers . . . like music-review artists talking and pouring strange liquors from curiously beautiful bottles . . . bottles with long slender necks . . . he climbed the noisy stair of the odorous tenement . . . smelled of fish . . . of stale fried fish and dirty milk bottles . . . he rather liked it . . . he liked the acrid smell of horse manure too . . . strong . . . thoughts . . . yes to lie back among strangely fashioned cushions and sip eastern wines and talk . . . Alex threw himself on the bed . . . removed his shoes . . . stretched and relaxed . . . yes and have music waft softly into the darkened and incensed room . . . he blew a cloud of smoke . . . oh the joy of being an artist and of blowing blue smoke thru an ivory holder inlaid with red jade and green . . .

the street was so long and narrow . . . so long and narrow . . . and blue . . . in the distance it reached the stars . . . and if he walked long enough . . . far enough . . . he could reach the stars too . . . the narrow blue was so empty . . . quiet . . . Alex walked music . . . it was nice to walk in the blue after a party . . . Zora had shone again . . . her stories . . . she always shone . . . and Monty was glad . . . every one was glad when Zora shone . . . he was glad he had gone to Monty's party . . . Monty had a nice place in the village . . . nice lights . . . and friends and wine . . . mother would be scandalized that he could think of going to a party . . . without a copper to his name . . . but then mother had never been to Monty's . . . and mother had never seen the street seem long and narrow and blue . . . Alex walked music . . . the click of his heels kept time with a tune in his mind . . . he glanced into a lighted cafe window . . . inside were people sipping coffee . . . men . . . why did they sit there in the loud light . . . didn't they know that outside the street . . . the narrow blue street met the stars . . . that if they walked long enough . . . far enough . . . Alex walked and the click of his heels sounded . . . and had an echo . . . sound being tossed back and forth . . . back and forth . . . some one was approaching . . . and their echoes mingled . . . and gave the sound of castenets . . . Alex liked the sound of the approaching man's footsteps . . . he walked music also . . . he knew the beauty of the narrow blue . . . Alex knew that by the way their echoes mingled . . . he wished he would speak . . . but strangers don't speak at four o'clock in the morning . . . at least if they did he couldn't imagine what would be said . . . maybe . . . pardon me but are you walking toward the stars . . . yes, sir, and if you walk long enough . . . then may I walk with you I want to reach the stars too . . . perdone me senor tiene vd. fosforo . . . Alex was glad he had been addressed in Spanish . . . to have been asked for a match in English . . . or to have been addressed in English at all . . . would have been blasphemy just then . . . Alex handed him a match . . . he glanced at his companion apprehensively in the match glow . . . he was afraid that his appearance would shatter the blue thoughts . . . and stars . . . ah . . . his face was a perfect compliment to his voice . . . and the echo of their steps mingled . . . they walked in silence . . . the castanets of their heels clicking accompaniment . . . the stranger inhaled deeply and with a nod of content and a smile . . . blew a cloud of smoke . . . Alex felt like singing . . . the stranger knew the magic of blue smoke also . . . they continued in silence . . . the castanets of their heels clicking rythmically . . . Alex turned in his doorway . . . up the stairs and the stranger waited for him to light the room . . . no need for words . . . they had always known each other . . . as they undressed by the blue dawn . . . Alex knew he had never seen a more perfect being . . . his body was all symmetry and music . . . and Alex called him Beauty . . . long they lay . . . blowing smoke and exchanging thoughts . . . and Alex swallowed with difficulty . . . he felt a glow of tremor . . . and they talked and . . . slept . . .

Alex wondered more and more why he liked Adrian so . . . he liked many people . . . Wallie . . . Zora . . . Clement . . . Gloria . . . Langston . . . John . . . Gwenny . . . oh many people . . . and they were friends . . . but Beauty . . . it was different . . . once Alex had admired Beauty's strength . . . and Beauty's eyes had grown soft and he had said . . . I like you more than any one Dulce . . . Adrian always called him Dulce . . . and Alex had become confused . . . was it that he was so susceptible to beauty that Alex liked Adrian so much . . . but no . . . he knew other people who were beautiful . . . Fania and Gloria . . . Monty and Bunny . . . but he was never confused before them . . . while Beauty . . . Beauty could make him believe in Buddha . . . or imps . . . and no one else could do that . . . that is no one but Melva . . . but then he was in love with Melva . . . and that explained that . . . he would like Beauty to know Melva . . . they were both so perfect . . . such compliments . . .

yes he would like Beauty to know Melva because he loved them both . . . there . . . he had thought it . . . actually dared to think it . . . but Beauty must never know . . . Beauty couldn't understand . . . indeed Alex couldn't understand . . . and it pained him . . . almost physically . . . and tired his mind . . . Beauty . . . Beauty was in the air . . . the smoke . . . Beauty . . . Melva . . . Beauty . . . Melva . . . Alex slept . . . and dreamed he was in a field . . . a field of blue smoke and black poppies and red calla lilies . . . he was searching . . . on his hands and knees . . . searching . . . among black poppies and red calla lilies . . . he was searching pushed aside poppy stems . . . and saw two strong white legs . . . dancer's legs . . . the contours pleased him . . . his eyes wandered . . . on past the muscular hocks to the firm white thighs . . . the rounded buttocks . . . then the lithe narrow waist . . . strong torso and broad deep chest . . . the heavy shoulders . . . the graceful muscled neck . . . squared chin and quizzical lips . . . grecian nose with its temperamental nostrils . . . the brown eyes looking at him . . . like . . . Monty looked at Zora . . . his hair curly and black and all tousled . . . and it was Beauty . . . and Beauty smiled and looked at him and smiled . . . said . . . I'll wait Alex . . . and Alex became confused and continued his search . . . on his hands and knees . . . pushing aside poppy stems and lily stems . . . a poppy . . . a black poppy . . . a lilly . . . a red lilly . . . and when he looked back he could no longer see Beauty . . . Alex continued his search . . . thru poppies . . . lilies . . . poppies and red calla lilies . . . and suddenly he saw . . . two small feet olive-ivory . . . two well turned legs curving gracefully from slender ankles . . . and the contours soothed him . . . he followed them . . . past the narrow rounded hips to the tiny waist . . . the fragile firm breasts . . . the graceful slender throat . . . the soft rounded chin . . . slightly parting lips and straight little nose with its slightly flaring nostrils . . . the black eyes with lights in them . . . looking at him . . . the forehead and straight cut black hair . . . and it was Melva . . . and she looked at him and smiled and said . . . I'll wait Alex . . . and Alex became confused and kissed her . . . became confused and continued his search . . . on his hands and knees . . . pushed aside a poppy stem . . . a black-poppy stem . . . pushed aside a lily stem . . . a red-lily stem . . . a poppy . . . a poppy . . . a lily . . . and suddenly he stood erect . . . exhultant . . . and in his hand he held . . . an ivory holder . . . inlaid with red jade . . . and green . . . .

and Alex awoke . . . Beauty's hair tickled his nose . . . Beauty was smiling in his sleep . . . half his face stained flush color by the sun . . . the other half in shadow . . . blue shadow . . . his eye lashes casting cobwebby blue shadows on his cheek . . . his lips were so beautiful . . . quizzical . . . Alex wondered why he always thought of that passage from Wilde's Salome . . . when he looked at Beauty's lips . . . I would kiss your lips . . . he *would* like to kiss Beauty's lips . . . Alex flushed warm . . . with shame . . . or was it shame . . . he reached across Beauty for a cigarette . . . Beauty's cheek felt cool to his arm . . . his hair felt soft . . . Alex lay smoking . . . such a dream . . . red calla lilies . . . red calla lilies . . . and . . . what could it all mean . . . did dreams have meanings . . . Fania said . . . and black poppies . . . thousands . . . millions . . . Beauty stirred . . . Alex put out his cigarette . . . closed his eyes . . . he mustn't see Beauty yet . . . speak to him . . . his lips were too hot . . . dry . . . the palms of his hands too cool and moist . . . thru his half closed eyes he could see Beauty . . . propped . . . cheek in hand . . . on one elbow . . . looking at him . . . lips smiling quizzically . . . he wished Beauty wouldn't look so hard . . . Alex was finding it difficult to breathe . . . breathe normally . . . why *must* Beauty look so long . . . and smile *that* way . . . his face seemed nearer . . . it was . . . Alex could feel Beauty's hair on his forehead . . . breathe normally . . . breathe normally . . . could feel Beauty's breath on his nostrils and lips . . . and it was clean and faintly colored with tobacco . . . breathe normally Alex . . . Beauty's lips were nearer . . . Alex closed his eyes . . . how did one act . . . his pulse was hammering . . . from wrists to finger tip . . . wrist to finger tip . . . Beauty's lips touched his . . . his temples throbbed . . . throbbed . . . his pulse hammered from wrist to finger tip . . . Beauty's breath came short now . . . softly staccato . . . breathe normally Alex . . . you are asleep . . . Beauty's lips touched his . . . breathe normally . . . and pressed . . . pressed hard . . . cool . . . his body trembled . . . breathe normally Alex . . . Beauty's lips pressed cool . . . cool and hard . . . how much pressure does it take to waken one . . . Alex sighed . . . moved softly . . . how does one act . . . Beauty's hair barely touched him now . . . his breath was faint on . . . Alex's nostrils . . . and lips . . . Alex stretched and opened his eyes . . . Beauty was looking at him . . . propped on one elbow . . . cheek in his palm . . . Beauty spoke . . . scratch my head please Dulce . . . Alex was breathing normally now . . . propped against the bed head . . . Beauty's head in his lap . . . Beauty spoke . . . I wonder why I like to look at some things Dulce . . . things like smoke and cats . . . and you . . . Alex's pulse no longer hammered from . . .

wrist to finger tip . . . wrist to finger tip . . . the rose dusk had become blue night . . . and soon . . . soon they would go out into the blue . . . .

the little church was crowded . . . warm . . . the rows of benches were brown and sticky . . . Harold was there . . . and Constance and Langston and Bruce and John . . . there was Mr. Robeson . . . how are you Paul . . . a young man was singing . . . Caver . . . Caver was a very self assured young man . . . such a dream . . . poppies . . . black poppies . . . they were applauding . . . Constance and John were exchanging notes . . . the benches were sticky . . . a young lady was playing the piano . . . fair . . . and red calla lilies . . . who had ever heard of red calla lilies . . . they were applauding . . . a young man was playing the viola . . . what could it all mean . . . so many poppies . . . and Beauty looking at him like . . . like Monty looked at Zora . . . another young man was playing a violin . . . he was the first real artist to perform . . . he had a touch of soul . . . or was it only feeling . . . they were hard to differentiate on the violin . . . and Melva standing in the poppies and lilies . . . Mr. Phillips was singing . . . Mr. Phillips was billed as a basso . . . and he had kissed her . . . they were applauding . . . the first young man was singing again . . . Langston's spiritual . . .

Fy-ah-fy-ah-Lawd . . . fy-ah's gonna burn ma soul . . . Beauty's hair was so black and curly . . . they were applauding . . . encore . . . Fy-ah Lawd had been a success . . . Langston bowed . . . Langston had written the words . . . Hall bowed . . . Hall had written the music . . . the young man was singing it again . . . Beauty's lips had pressed hard . . . cool . . . cool . . . fy-ah Lawd . . . his breath had trembled . . . fy-ah's gonna burn ma soul . . . they were all leaving . . . first to the roof dance . . . fy-ah Lawd . . . there was Catherine . . . she was beautiful tonight . . . she always was at night . . . Beauty's lips . . . fy-ah Lawd . . . hello Dot . . . why don't you take a boat that sails . . . when are you leaving again . . . and there's Estelle . . . every one was there . . . fy-ah Lawd . . . Beauty's body had pressed close . . . close . . . fy-ah's gonna burn my soul . . . let's leave . . . have to meet some people at the New World . . . then to Augusta's party . . . Harold . . . John . . . Bruce . . . Connie . . . Langston . . . ready . . . down one hundred thirty-fifth street . . . fy-ah . . . meet these people and leave . . . fy-ah Lawd . . . now to Augusta's party . . . fy-ahs gonna burn ma soul . . . they were at Augusta's . . . Alex half lay . . . half sat on the floor . . . sipping a cocktail . . . such a dream . . . red calla lilies . . . Alex left . . . down the narrow streets . . .

fy-ah . . . up the long noisy stairs . . . fy-ahs gonna bu'n ma soul . . . his head felt swollen . . . expanding . . . contracting . . . expanding . . . contracting . . . he had never been like this before . . . expanding . . . contracting . . . it was that . . . fy-ah . . . fy-ah Lawd . . . and the cocktails . . . and Beauty . . . he felt two cool strong hands on his shoulders . . . it was Beauty . . . lie down Dulce . . . Alex lay down . . . Beauty . . . Alex stopped . . . no no . . . don't say it . . . Beauty mustn't know . . . Beauty couldn't understand . . . are you going to lie down too Beauty . . . the light went out expanding . . . contracting . . . he felt the bed sink as Beauty lay beside him . . . his lips were dry . . . hot . . . the palms of his hands so moist and cool . . . Alex partly closed his eyes . . . from beneath his lashes he could see Beauty's face over his . . . nearer . . . nearer . . . Beauty's hair touched his forehead now . . . he could feel his breath on his nostrils and lips . . . Beauty's breath came short . . . breathe normally Beauty . . . breathe normally . . . Beauty's lips touched his . . . pressed hard . . . cool . . . opened slightly . . . Alex opened his eyes . . . into Beauty's . . . parted his lips . . . Dulce . . . Beauty's breath was hot and short . . . Alex ran his hand through Beauty's hair . . . Beauty's lips pressed hard against his teeth . . . Alex trembled . . . could feel

Beauty's body . . . close against his . . . hot . . . tense . . . white . . . and soft . . . soft . . . soft . . . .

they were at Forno's . . . every one came to Forno's once maybe only once . . . but they came . . . see that big fat woman Beauty . . . Alex pointed to an overly stout and bejeweled lady making her way thru the maize of chairs . . . that's Maria Guerrero . . . Beauty looked to see a lady guiding almost the whole opera company to an immense table . . . really Dulce . . . for one who appreciates beauty you do use the most abominable English . . . Alex lit a cigarette . . . and that florid man with white hair . . . that's Carl . . . Beauty smiled . . . The Blind bow boy . . . he asked . . . Alex wondered . . . everything seemed to . . . so just the same . . . here they were laughing and joking about people . . . there's Rene . . . Rene this is my friend Adrian . . . after that night . . . and he felt so unembarrassed . . . Rene and Adrian were talking . . . there was Lucricia Bori . . . she was bowing at their table . . . oh her cousin was with them . . . and Peggy Joyce . . . every one came to Forno's . . . Alex looked toward the door . . . there was Melva . . . Alex beckoned . . . Melva this is Adrian . . . Beauty held her hand . . .

Smoke, Lilies and Jade

they talked . . . smoked . . . Alex loved Melva . . . in Forno's . . . every one came there sooner or later . . . maybe once . . . but . . . .

up . . . up . . . slow . . . jerk up . . . up . . . not fast . . . not glorious . . . but slow . . . up . . . up into the sun . . . slow . . . sure like fate . . . poise on the brim . . . the brim of life . . . two shining rails straight down . . . Melva's head was on his shoulder . . . his arm was around her . . . poise . . . the down . . . gasping . . . straight down . . . straight like sin . . . down . . . the curving shiny rail rushed up to meet them . . . hit the bottom then . . . shoot up . . . fast . . . glorious . . . up into the sun . . . Melva gasped . . . Alex's arm tightened . . . all goes up . . . then down . . . straight like hell . . . all breath squeezed out of them . . . Melva's head on his shoulder . . . up . . . up . . . Alex kissed her . . . down . . . they stepped out of the car . . . walking music . . . now over to the Ferris Wheel . . . out and up . . . Melva's hand was soft in his . . . out and up . . . over mortals . . . mortals drinking nectar . . . five cents a glass . . . her cheek was soft on his . . . up . . . up . . . till the world seemed small . . . tiny . . . the ocean seemed tiny and blue . . . up . . . up and out . . . over the sun . . . the tiny red sun . . . Alex kissed her . . . up . . . up . . .

their tongues touched . . . up . . . seventh heaven . . . the sea had swallowed the sun . . . up and out . . . her breath was perfumed . . . Alex kissed her . . . drift down . . . soft . . . soft . . . the sun had left the sky flushed . . . drift down . . . soft down . . . back to earth . . . visit the mortals sipping nectar at five cents a glass . . . Melva's lips brushed his . . . then out among the mortals . . and the sun had left a flush on Melva's cheeks . . . they walked hand in hand . . . and the moon came out . . . they walked in silence on the silver strip . . . and the sea sang for them . . . they walked toward the moon . . . we'll hang our hats on the crook of the moon Melva . . . softly on the silver strip . . . his hands molded her features and her cheeks were soft and warm to his touch . . . where is Adrian . . . Alex . . . Melva trod silver . . . Alex trod sand . . . Alex trod sand . . . the sea *sang* for her . . . Beauty . . . her hand felt cold in his . . . Beauty . . . the sea *dinned* . . . Beauty . . . he led the way to the train . . . and the train dinned . . . Beauty . . . dinned . . . dinned . . . her cheek *had* been soft . . . Beauty . . . Beauty . . . her breath *had* been perfumed . . . Beauty . . . Beauty . . . the sands *had* been silver . . . Beauty . . . Beauty . . . they left the train . . . Melva walked music . . . Melva said . . . don't make me blush again . . . and kissed him . . . Alex stood on the steps after she left him and the night was black . . . down long streets to . . . Alex lit a cigarette . . . and his heels clicked . . . Beauty . . . Melva . . . Beauty . . . Melva . . . and the smoke made the night blue . . .

Melva had said . . . don't make me blush again . . . and kissed him . . . and the street had been blue . . . one *can* love two at the same time . . . Melva had kissed him . . . one *can* . . . and the street had been blue . . . one *can* . . . and the room was clouded with blue smoke . . . drifting vapors of smoke and thoughts . . . Beauty's hair was so black . . . and soft . . . blue smoke from an ivory holder . . . was that why he loved Beauty . . . one *can* . . . or because his body was beautiful . . . and white and warm . . . or because his eyes . . . one *can* love . . . .

RICHARD BRUCE.

. . . To Be Continued . . .

Permissions Acknowledgements

Extract from 'Boy' by Langston Hughes from *The Collected Poems of Langston Hughes* (Alfred A. Knopf Inc.); reproduced by permission of David Higham Associates.

'Enoch Soames' by Max Beerbohm reproduced by permission of Berlin Associates Ltd. as the agent for the Beerbohm Estate.

Translation of 'Funeral Oration' (*Oraison funèbre*) by Jean Lorrain copyright © Jane Desmarais 2011.

MACMILLAN COLLECTOR'S LIBRARY

Own the world's great works of literature in one beautiful collectible library

Designed and curated to appeal to book lovers everywhere, Macmillan Collector's Library editions are small enough to travel with you and striking enough to take pride of place on your bookshelf. These much-loved literary classics also make the perfect gift.

Beautifully made, every Macmillan Collector's Library book adheres to the same high production values. Each hardback features gilt edges, a ribbon marker and cloth binding, and every paperback has a bespoke illustrated cover.

Discover a new and exciting anthology or cherish your favourite classic stories with this elegant collection.

Macmillan Collector's Library: own, collect, and treasure

Discover the full range at
panmacmillan.com/mcl